"It's time to talk about your future, Joanna," Kirk announced.

"That has all the appeal of a five-year jail term. You make it sound like I'm a new type of lawn chair you're planning to market," Joanna retorted.

"Nobody in his right mind would mistake you for a lawn chair." His eyes wandered down her curves.

"See anything you like?"

Kirk barely held on to his temper. "What am I going to do with you? I'm your guardian, and the caretaker of your money until you're thirty."

"Or until I'm married."

"Do you have somebody in mind?"

The answer popped out before Joanna could stop it. "You."

Kirk gave her a look of such intensity that she felt as if she were melting inside. She felt herself drowning in his eyes, falling hopelessly into the passion she saw there. Warning bells clanged in her mind, and she heard the voice of reason. Joanna Deerfield and Kirk Maitland? Impossible. It would be like hitching a mountain to a tornado....

Dear Reader,

Welcome to Silhouette—experience the magic of the wonderful world where two people fall in love. Meet heroines that will make you cheer for their happiness, and heroes (be they the boy next door or a handsome, mysterious stranger) who will win your heart. Silhouette Romance reflects the magic of love—sweeping you away with books that will make you laugh and cry, heartwarming, poignant stories that will move you time and time again.

In the coming months we're publishing romances by many of your all-time favorites, such as Diana Palmer, Brittany Young, Sondra Stanford and Annette Broadrick. Your response to these authors and our other Silhouette Romance authors has served as a touchstone for us, and we're pleased to bring you more books with Silhouette's distinctive medley of charm, wit and—above all—*romance*.

I hope you enjoy this book and the many stories to come. Experience the magic!

Sincerely,

Tara Hughes
Senior Editor
Silhouette Books

PEGGY WEBB

When Joanna Smiles

Published by Silhouette Books New York

America's Publisher of Contemporary Romance

SILHOUETTE BOOKS
300 E. 42nd St., New York, N.Y. 10017

ISBN: 0-373-08645-8

First Silhouette Books printing April 1989

Printed in the U.S.A.

PEGGY WEBB

grew up in a large northeastern Mississippi family in which the Southern tradition of storytelling was elevated to an art. "In our family there was always a romance or a divorce or a scandal going on," she says, "and always someone willing to tell it. By the time I was thirteen I knew I would be a writer."

Over the years Peggy has raised her two children—and twenty-five dogs. "Any old stray is welcome," she acknowledges. "My house is known as Dog Heaven." Recently her penchant for trying new things led her to take karate lessons. Although she was the oldest person in her class and one of only two women, she now has a blue belt in tansai karate. Her karate practice came to a halt, though, when wrens built a nest in her punching bag. "I decided to take up bird-watching," says Peggy.

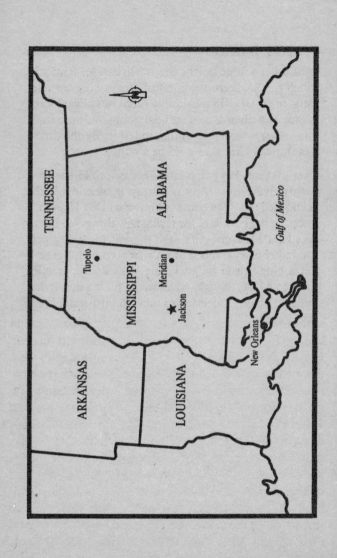

Chapter One

I get out of prison tomorrow.''

Joanna held the phone away so Kirk's reply couldn't scorch her ear. Near the window, Sister Maria Teresa clutched her Rosary beads and beseeched the ceiling. Praying for patience, no doubt, Joanna thought. Either that or hoping for a last-minute miracle to reform the most reluctant student ever sent to set foot inside the Santa Maria Magdalena Colegio y Conservatorio de Arte y Musica. Joanna felt a small twinge of guilt. Poor old soul. She'd done her best; all the nuns had. It wasn't that Joanna didn't like them and didn't appreciate the fine education she'd received in Madrid. It was simply that she was tired of being told what to do. No, ordered. Her guardian, Kirk Maitland, didn't tell; he gave orders. And there were so many rules at the school that she could break one without even trying. Being a natural-born rebel hadn't helped, either.

When the explosive response at the other end of the line died down, Joanna put the receiver back to her ear.

"I was hoping that four years of study abroad would tame you," Kirk was saying.

"Tame me? Is that why you put an ocean between us? Because I'm not tame enough for Tupelo, Mississippi? Or was that dear old Belinda's suggestion? No sooner had she pranced into Meadowlane than you shipped me off."

"Belinda had nothing to do with the decision, and you know it. I thought you wanted to study art at the Prado. Besides, the Spanish society is protective of young girls. I did it for your own good."

"I'm not a girl; I'm a woman. And I'm smothering to death in good intentions."

There was a long pause at the other end of the line. Joanna could picture Kirk, his gray eyes cool and alert, his dark hair short and neat, pondering the matter with the same intensity he brought to his board meetings. Kirk never did or said an impulsive thing—unless Joanna had provoked him to an uncharacteristic rage.

"Joanna, there's no need for you to feel that way. We'll discuss this matter when you get home," he finally said.

She decided the time was right to break her big news, the main reason she'd called. "I have a problem, Kirk. But it's just a small one."

"You said that when you were in Morocco and gave all your money to a con man who passed himself off as a penniless camel driver trying to feed a hungry family. Somehow I don't feel reassured."

"That was two summers ago. This problem is not about money. For once in my life, my bank account is bulging with pesetas. My small problem is that I'm not coming home."

There was a pregnant silence on Kirk's end of the line. She could imagine him, planning his arguments, planning her future. She hurried on before he could get his thoughts organized. "Some friends and I are going down to Marbella. We're going to bum around the Costa del Sol for a while, further our liberal education."

"Dammit, Joanna. I worry about you. You're a babe in the woods, a wide-eyed innocent who would give the shirt off your back to anybody with a sob story. What am I going to do with you?"

She chuckled. "Give me a credit card?"

"You'd buy New York." She heard his resigned sigh, the sound of a man who knows he's fighting a losing battle. "When are you coming home?"

"When my money runs out. A few weeks, Kirk. Maybe longer. Don't worry about me."

"Promise me one thing, Joanna."

"What?"

"Be careful."

She crossed her fingers behind her back. "I will. See you, Kirk." As she hung up, she didn't feel the least bit guilty about the lie. Being careful was the last thing on her mind. She'd had four years of being told what to do by the nuns. Before that, Kirk had watched over her. Not that she blamed him for being protective. She supposed it came from long habit.

She remembered the first time they'd ever met. She'd been three. The entire family had gathered at Meadowlane to meet Aunt Sophie, her new husband, Kenneth Maitland, and her new stepson, Kirk. Grandfather Deerfield had been sitting in his favorite high-backed rocking chair on the front porch, sipping a mint julep, listening to Bach through his radio earphones and conducting the imaginary orchestra with dramatic waves of his hand. Joanna's mother had been flitting in and out the front door, fussing over the refreshments, the flower arrangements and the deteriorating state of Joanna's white pinafore. And Joanna had been clutching three buttercups to give to her brand-new cousin.

When the big moment came to give the flowers to Kirk, their pitiful heads had lolled on broken stems. Joanna had burst into tears. She would never forget what had happened next. Kirk had bent over her, patted her curls and told her he could fix them. And he had. When he'd taped the broken stems and closed her tiny fist around them, she'd fallen in love as fiercely as her three-year-old heart would allow.

Kirk had been fixing things for her ever since.

But she was no longer three; she was twenty-two and determined to do things her way—for once in her life.

"We will miss you, Joanna."

Sister Maria Teresa's voice brought her out of her reverie. Her English was nearly as perfect as her Spanish.

Joanna smiled. "I would have thought you'd be glad to get rid of me."

Sister Maria Teresa laughed. "The Lord moves in mysterious ways. I think he used your liveliness to keep some of us old froggies on our toes."

"Old fogies, Sister."

"See what I mean? Who will correct my slang when you're gone?" She surreptitiously dabbed at her eyes.

Joanna walked over and hugged her. "Maybe the Lord will send you another Southern rebel."

Still trying to hide her feelings in laughter, Sister Maria Teresa walked Joanna through the cool stone corridor to the gates of the college; but Joanna saw the tears slide down her cheek and tunnel through the lines of her dear old face.

"I'll write." She said it on impulse, perhaps as a way to atone for all the mischief she'd caused.

"In Spanish, Joanna." Sister Maria Teresa wiped her tears openly now, and tried to look stern. "You must keep in practice."

"*Sí, tu amigo.*"

Joanna gave her one last hug, then picked up her suitcase and walked through the gates.

Joanna's money lasted till June. She left Marbella on a sunny afternoon, flying with the sun, gaining time so that she arrived in Tupelo at dusk. When the plane touched down on Mississippi soil, she thought she'd cry. It had been four years since she'd been home, four years in exile—although an exile partly of her own choosing, she had to admit. After Kirk had married Belinda, Meadowlane was never the same. Vacations and holidays, Joanna had chosen to travel in Europe rather than face the altered state of affairs at home. Even after the divorce two years ago she still hadn't come home. She'd learned to love travel—seeing new places, meeting new people. The freedom had appealed to her, too. When she'd traveled she'd been a vagabond, with no nuns to tell her how long to wear her skirt and no guardian to tell her how late to stay out.

But now she was back. And she was glad.

Joanna picked up her luggage, rented a car and headed home. Home was Meadowlane, the Deerfield family mansion set on a sloping green hillside on the outskirts of Tupelo. A lump came into her throat as she lifted her eyes to the huge white columns and wide verandas. It had been home to her since she could remember. Shortly after Aunt Sophie had married Kenneth Maitland, Joanna's father, Roger Deerfield, had been killed in a freak accident. Her mother, Janet, being the flighty type, had mostly left her in the care of Grandfather Deerfield. He'd become her legal guardian, with Janet's full approval; and at his death six years ago, he'd passed that job on to Kirk Maitland. Kirk had also been named executor of the Deerfield fortune. Meadowlane had been left to his only grandchildren—Joanna and Kirk.

Looking at Meadowlane now, remembering how it used to be when her parents were alive, Joanna felt the old hurt and bewilderment arise. She didn't know what had prompted her mother to give her up, to leave Meadowlane. She used to wonder if she'd done something wrong, something so bad her mother had to leave.

Firmly she squelched those thoughts. She was home now, and nothing else mattered.

Joanna parked the rented Ford in the four-car garage beside a black Lincoln and a navy Oldsmobile. Steady, reliable cars. Just the kind Kirk would choose. Personally, she preferred flashy cars in bright colors, Jaguars and Porsches and Corvettes in shocking red and neon blue and even passionate purple. Slinging her Louis Vuitton bag over her shoulder, she got out of the car and walked around to the front of the house. No wonder she and Kirk never saw eye to eye on anything. They were as different as Alaska and Arkansas—and just about as far apart.

She squared her jaw in an unconsciously rebellious gesture. She was a grown woman now, and she was determined to take charge of her own life. Guardian or no, Kirk Maitland might as well get ready to hand over the reins. She figured it would be a battle royal, but she was equal to the task.

Opening the front door, she walked into the hallway, both guns blazing.

She found Kirk sitting in his study, door cracked open, apparently so absorbed in his work he hadn't heard her come in. The first sight of him so captivated her that she barely noticed Rags, the little cocker spaniel, asleep near the hearth. Kirk looked older, she thought. But the gray at his temples and the fine network of lines fanning out from his eyes didn't diminish his charm in the least. In fact, they only added to it. In four years she had almost forgotten that devastating charm.

Unconsciously her tongue flicked out and wet her dry lips. Kirk Maitland always had been and still was the best-looking man she'd ever seen. As usual, he was well groomed and immaculate, every inch the successful businessman; but he was also fit and tanned, with enough muscle to show he was not desk-bound and not so much that he looked overdone, as if he could bench-press Texas.

Joanna hesitated in the doorway. The way he looked didn't help her cause one bit. She'd been prepared to march straight into battle, but all she wanted to do at the moment was march straight into his arms—just the way she'd been doing since she was three years old. She sighed. Old habits died hard.

"I'm home."

Kirk's head jerked up. "Joanna!"

The intense pleasure of his smile almost made her forget her recent intention to declare war. He rose from his desk and strode toward her. At first she thought he meant to scoop her into his arms for a friendly bear hug, the way he always had, but when he was only inches from her, he stopped.

"Your hair." He lifted his hand as if he meant to touch it, then let it drop to his side. "It's different."

Joanna raked her hand through her short red curls. "I'm too old for a ponytail. My freckles have faded, too."

"I noticed."

But he wasn't noticing her freckles; he was looking at the way her breasts pushed against the front of her silk blouse. Joanna felt a wicked glee at his obvious discomfiture. It was high time Kirk Maitland knew he was dealing with a woman.

"I never had freckles there."

He lifted his gaze with such alacrity she almost giggled. "Joanna, you always were the most exasperating female I ever knew." He turned and practically stomped back to his desk. "Where are your bags?"

"In the car."

"I'll have Roger take them up to your room." He pressed the intercom and gave his instructions.

Taking charge, as always, Joanna thought. She'd been home less than ten minutes, and already Kirk was making decisions for her.

"How do you know I'll be staying in my room?" She never had any intention of staying anywhere else, but perversity and desire for battle made her ask.

"This is your home. Of course you'll be staying here."

"I'll stay where I good and damned well please."

"Where did you learn such language?"

"That school you shipped me off to. I can now cuss in four languages."

She saw the beginning of his smile, saw him struggle to squelch his laughter. Oh, Lord, help me, she thought. Don't let him laugh. She'd always loved the way he laughed, full-bodied, head thrown back. If he laughed now, she might get sidetracked from her purpose. It was hard to do battle with someone who was laughing.

"Where do you intend to stay, Joanna?" The hint of laughter was gone, and that cool, calm manner of his was back. Joanna felt an urge to smash something. "You told me yourself that you'd be home when your money ran out.

Even with your winning and enterprising ways, I don't think you can find lodging without money."

"I'll think of something—tomorrow. Right now I have jet lag. I'm going upstairs to rest."

She saw his face soften. His voice was soft, too, when he spoke. Gruff and tender. "I'm sorry, baby. I know you must be tired. Welcome home, Joanna."

She knew that tenderness would be her undoing if she didn't take quick action. Never one to look before she leaped, she hurried across the room to him. "You've always welcomed me home with a kiss." Leaning over his chair, she kissed him full on the mouth. She felt his stillness, his resistance. She felt something else, too. The compelling power of him. It pulsed beneath her lips, an explosiveness that he kept carefully leashed. Excitement surged through her, and on its heels, bewilderment.

She had meant the kiss to be a victory on her part, a triumphant display of her womanhood and independence. Instead it threatened to be her downfall. She had wanted to shock Kirk, not set herself into a fine state of confusion. Quickly she pulled back and hurried from the room.

She marched up the stairs, taking a perverse satisfaction from stomping loudly on the steps. That was just round one. Her battle flags were at half-mast, and her big guns hadn't even been fired, but her war for freedom was just beginning.

After Joanna left the room, Kirk sat, stunned, in his chair. He felt like a man who had been invited to a banquet and discovered that he was going to be the main dish. My God. Where had she learned to kiss like that? He'd had a hell of a time to keep from kissing her back. In an uncharacteristic gesture of frustration, he raked his hands through his hair. Joanna knew damned well he'd never welcomed her home with more than a peck on the cheek. Who had taught her that stuff anyhow? Some damned foreigner, most likely. Out to take advantage of her youth and innocence. He felt the urge to kill. A paternal urge, of course, he assured himself.

Forcing himself to calm down, he picked up the work he'd brought home from the office. It claimed his attention for two minutes, then his mind was back on Joanna. He decided the best thing to do was take a day off from business so he could help her settle in and get her future planned. The sooner she was safely taken care of, the better off they'd all be.

Kirk was waiting in the sun room when Joanna awakened the next day.

She walked in, her smile as bright as the yellow sundress she was wearing. If he'd flown from Spain yesterday, he thought, he would still be dragging. Suddenly he felt old—and extremely conscious of the span of thirteen years that separated them.

"Good morning, Joanna. I assumed you'd sleep late, so I had Rose prepare brunch." He nodded toward the glass-top table.

She slid into the seat across the table from him. "As usual, you're taking care of me."

That rebellious note he'd detected yesterday was still in her voice. It was uncharacteristic of Joanna. As a child she'd always had such a sunny disposition. But then, she was no longer a child. She'd made that uncomfortably clear yesterday.

"Did you sleep well?"

"Yes. Did you?"

"Yes." Small talk, he thought. Something he and Joanna had never had to resort to. He watched her eat her meal. She had the healthy appetite of youth. Belinda had been like her in so many ways. Vivacious, fun-loving, full of laughter. And ten years younger than he. Theirs had been one of the shortest, most disastrous marriages in history. She'd said he stifled her, and he'd claimed she wanted to change him. Neither of them would give an inch.

He was glad that unlikely alliance was behind him. It was a mistake he never intended repeating. If he ever took the marital plunge again—which wasn't likely, considering he was so busy with business—it damned sure wouldn't be with a younger woman.

"You've grown solemn in your old age." The twinkle in Joanna's dark eyes told him she was teasing. "Or is your dark brooding due to lack of female companionship?"

Her sly little grin made him laugh. "If that's your not-so-subtle way of asking if I keep a woman in my bed, the answer is 'none of your business'."

"I was hoping for a few salacious details. To further my liberal education, you know."

Kirk thought her chuckle was positively wicked. And undeniably charming. He took a fortifying gulp of coffee and decided to change the subject.

"It's time to talk about your future, Joanna."

Her expression shifted from laughter to indignation, and Kirk felt a twinge of regret.

"That has all the appeal of a five-year jail term. You make it sound like I'm a new type of aluminum lawn chair you're planning to market at Deerfield Manufacturing."

"Nobody in his right mind would mistake you for a lawn chair." He hadn't meant his eyes to wander down her new curves, but they did. And damn the luck, she noticed.

"See anything you like?"

Kirk barely held on to his temper. "Who taught you such outrageous behavior?"

"Would you believe the nuns?"

"Joanna. My God, what am I going to do with you?"

"Nothing. I'm going to do it all myself."

"I'm your guardian, and the caretaker of your money until you're thirty."

"Or until I'm married."

"Do you have somebody in mind?"

"You." The answer popped out before Joanna could stop it. And she didn't have any idea where it had come from.

Kirk gave her a look of such intensity that she felt as if she were melting inside. To cover her confusion, she began to chatter. "Who can think of a thing with you looking like that? Good grief, the expression on your face is enough to make saints take to cussing. Stop scowling, Kirk."

"I'm not scowling."

"Yes, you are. And now you're shouting."

She watched him look out the window, as if he were taking strength from the unchangeable earth of Meadowlane. When he turned back to her, he was maddeningly calm. He even took up his fork and ate a bite of ham before speaking to her again.

"You didn't answer my question, Joanna. If you have in mind that bullfighter you were so crazy about, may I remind you that their glory is short-lived? He'd never be able to take care of you the way he should."

"I discovered he likes pistachio nuts. I can't abide a man who likes pistachio nuts. Besides, that was last year. I've gone on to bigger and better things."

"Bigger and better? Joanna, I ought to turn you across my knee and spank you."

She threw back her head and laughed. "I think that piece of ham is dead now, Kirk."

"What?"

"You've stabbed it into submission with your fork. I think it's safe to eat now."

He put his fork down and leaned back in his chair. "Enough of this frivolity. It's time to do some serious talking. Have you decided what you want to do with your life?"

He was asking this time instead of telling. Joanna considered that a good sign. Maybe the simple truth could accomplish what sparring could not.

"There's a big world out there, Kirk. I want to see it all, every tree and flower and shrub, every stream and valley and mountain. I want to meet new people and discover new artists and hear great symphonies before anybody else even knows they exist. I want to grab life with both hands, and then when I'm old—over thirty-five—*then* I'll think about my future." She looked across the table and smiled.

"When you smile like that, Joanna, I swear I'd lay the world at your feet if I could. With the stars and moon thrown in for good measure." He lifted his coffee cup, never taking his eyes off her as he drank. When he put the cup down and started to speak, there was a hard edge of command in his voice, like steel clashing against steel. "I'm responsible for you. Travel is fine as a hobby, but not as a way of life. Grandfather Deerfield put his trust in me, treated me like his own flesh and blood. He and I often talked about your future. He wanted you to settle down in Tupelo, to become a part of Deerfield Manufacturing."

"I'd smother to death in aluminum lawn chairs and patio tables and board meetings and balance sheets."

"How do you know until you try it?"

"I *know*, Kirk. Trust me."

"How about your art? Have you ever thought of teaching or opening your own studio?"

"No. I will not let you run my life."

"I'm not running your life; I'm helping you make sensible choices."

She felt her future slipping from her hands. As usual, Kirk was taking charge. And as usual, she acted on impulse.

"You're giving orders. And I won't tolerate it. Kirk Maitland, I'm *not* going to bury myself in Deerfield Manufacturing and I'm *not* going to teach. I'm going to..." she hesitated only a second before saying the first place that popped into her head "...Siberia."

Kirk was tolerant with Joanna only up to a point. He'd reached that point now. He stalked around the table and lifted her out of her chair. Grasping her shoulders, he pulled her so close she could see the tiny scar on his jaw. "No, you're not. You're going to stay right here at Meadowlane—" He broke off abruptly, his eyes burning fiercely into hers.

For a breathless moment she thought he was going to kiss her. Returning his look, she felt herself drowning in his eyes, falling hopelessly into the whirlpool of passion she saw there. Warning bells clanged in her mind, and she heard the distant voice of reason. Joanna Deerfield and Kirk Maitland? Impossible. It would be like hitching a mountain to a tornado.

She drew herself up to her full height, tipped her head back and looked him squarely in the eye. "You can't keep me here."

"Yes, I can. You have no money. Remember?"

"If I did, I wouldn't spend it on aluminum lawn chairs. I'd spend it on a buttercup."

His face softened. "Joanna, be reasonable."

When Kirk looked at her like that, she had a hard time being mad at him. But her future was at stake. Courageously Joanna summoned up a royal anger. It was the only emotion strong enough to get her past her own strange and bewildering feelings. She didn't know exactly what she was going to do or say, but she was sure it would come to her.

"I'm not going to stay here and become a lady just because you and Grandfather planned it." Her eyes sparkled as she got into the act. She enjoyed her rages the same way she did everything else, wholeheartedly.

"I'm going to be myself..." she hesitated, inventing as she talked, "...starting in Siberia...tomorrow. And after that I'm going to Marbella and Monte Carlo and Barcelona and...I might even join a circus."

Kirk didn't even try to hide his smile. "How do you propose to do all that?"

"I'm going to get married."

Although she hadn't planned to say such a thing, once she'd said it she was too stubborn to back down. Besides, the idea had its merits. She couldn't think what they were right now, but she was sure she'd think of some later.

"My God, Joanna. You can't just get married. You have to fall in love first."

She waved her hands airily. "That'll be easy. I fell in love with you at least fifteen times when I was growing up. It shouldn't be too hard to find somebody to fall in love with."

"You're going to just pick somebody off the street and fall in love with him?"

"You don't have to roar."

"I'm not roaring."

"Yes, you are."

"People don't get married on the spur of the moment. They meet somebody suitable and after a decent courtship they fall in love. Marriage is a lifetime commitment. It takes forethought and planning." He scowled at her, then his face softened. Leaning down, he placed a tender kiss on her cheek. "Be reasonable, sweetheart. You can't just go out and drag some man to the altar."

She flashed a smile at him as a new idea took hold. "I don't intend to do that. You're going to find somebody for me. You've always fixed things for me."

His grip tightened on her shoulders. "No. I will not be a part of this insanity."

"Then I'll find my own husband."

Joanna jerked out of his grasp and whirled away from him. Her bare feet made smart slapping sounds on the tiles as she marched out of the sun room.

"Joanna, come back here," Kirk yelled, but she kept on walking. She had already decided who her first candidate would be, and she didn't have a minute to lose.

Kirk sat back down with the air of a man who had just experienced Pearl Harbor. He felt numb and rejuvenated at the same time. Furthermore, he couldn't decide if the warm glow he felt in his stomach was ulcers or desire. God knew, Joanna was desirable enough to make saints turn in their crowns.

From long habit, he set out to analyze the problem. He loved a challenge, and he'd never yet seen a problem that didn't have an answer. But as much as he racked his brain, he'd be damned if he could decide what had just happened there.

The sounds of Joanna drifted into the sun room; her voice lifted in sultry song, the slamming of the refrigerator door, a pregnant silence, then her heartfelt swearing. Kirk smiled. In the long run it really didn't matter what he was feeling at the moment, he decided. There was no need even to try and untangle his own conflicting emotions. Joanna was the issue here; she had been entrusted to him. Her happiness and future were of the utmost importance. He'd climb mountains, build kingdoms, slay dragons for her. She was special, and she needed a very special man, someone as witty and spontaneous and joyful as she.

He'd watch over her, just as he always had.

Chapter Two

Joanna had left the parlor door wide open.

Kirk considered walking across the hallway to close it, then decided he'd leave it open so he could keep an eye on her. True to her word, she was in the parlor with a prospective bridegroom, Wexford Wainwright, one of her former classmates. One of the least attractive ones, he noted with some satisfaction.

The sound of her happy laughter drifted across the hallway and into his study. He looked toward the parlor and saw her cross her legs, lifting her skirts so Wexford could get a good view. He felt an insane urge to go across the hall and punch the man in the face. He thought she winked, but he couldn't be sure. With Joanna one was never sure.

Kirk bent over his desk to work on the designs for a new sports chair, but not before he'd noticed Joanna's legs. Poor hapless Wexford. He didn't stand a chance. Kirk thought that it was a good thing he'd decided to work in his study tonight so he could keep an eye on her. There was no telling what she would do next.

He grinned. With Joanna life was a surprise party, complete with bazookas and drums and confetti. Reluctantly he dragged his mind away from her and focused on his designs, concentrating on the intricacies of creation. Then he heard Joanna speak, her outrageous words carrying clearly across the hall as if they'd been piped in by stereo.

"In Paris one never bothers with convention. One merely seizes the moment."

He jerked his head up in time to see her seizing the moment by draping herself around Wexford and practically wallowing in his lap. He stood up so fast his chair nearly toppled over. He wasn't about to sit back and see her marry a man who had failed second grade, even if Wexford had tried to redeem himself by growing up and taking Joanna to the senior prom.

Kirk was halfway across the room before his common sense reasserted itself. What was he going to do? Bounce the man out the door? Joanna was twenty-two. If she wanted to throw herself at some simpleton, that was her business. He couldn't be her keeper forever. Let her go ahead and marry the idiot. He'd be around to pick up the pieces when it was all over.

Feeling rather self-righteous and noble, he started back to his desk. Then Joanna laughed again. The sound spurred him to action. His shoes clapped smartly against the polished wooden floors as he stalked across his study and marched across the hall. Sticking his head around the parlor door, he inquired with elaborate politeness, "I'm going to have a glass of iced tea. Would anyone care to join me?"

Joanna unfolded herself from Wexford and gave him that bewitching smile she'd been practicing on him since she was three, the one that made him want to tuck her under his arm and protect her from the world.

"No, thank you, dahling. We're not hot enough for tea...yet."

He wanted to throttle her. *Dahling*, indeed. Not hot enough for tea...yet. He turned and practically stomped to the kitchen, but not before he'd pinned Wexford to the sofa with a deadly glare that made him turn Joanna loose.

Kirk punished the kitchen cabinets, banging the doors so hard the crystal goblets rattled on their fragile stems and threatened to topple off the shelves. He rummaged through the shelves, passing over his favorite iced-tea glass twice before he saw it, sitting in plain view on the front of the shelf. "Hell of a place to put a glass," he muttered as he snatched it and plopped it on the kitchen counter. Next he abused the refrigerator, jerking open the door so hard the tray of freshly formed cubes slid to the floor and dumped ice on his feet.

"Damned gadgets," he muttered as he bent to clean up the mess. "I tried to tell her, but would she listen? No. She's bound and determined to find herself a husband. Went out and picked the first fool she could find, that idiot who couldn't even find his way out of the sandpile at her fourth birthday party."

"Talking to yourself?"

He jerked his head up to see Joanna leaning against the doorway, looking as fresh and innocent as if she'd never tried to vamp poor Wexford out of his pants.

"What are you doing here? I thought you were busy courting that poor Wainwright fool?"

His irritation was increased by the weather. It was so sultry outside even the night birds weren't singing.

"I changed my mind about the tea."

She skirted around the ice and got a goblet from the cabinet.

"What about Wainwright?"

She stepped breezily through the ice and reached over him to the refrigerator. "I changed my mind about him, too."

Kirk stood up and dumped the ice into the sink. Her news improved his temper considerably.

"If you're looking for ice, I spilled it all on the floor. We'll have to wait for the ice maker to kick out some more."

"That's okay. I'll just pour myself some o.j." She tipped the cold pewter pitcher and poured herself a generous glass of orange juice. Looking up at him, she smiled. "Want some?"

"Yes. I'll have some." Holding out his glass, he realized that he'd missed her. Meadowlane was never the same when she was gone. Maybe it was that bright red hair, or the bouncy way she walked, or that voice, sometimes cheerful, sometimes throaty, and sometimes lifted in a fine rage. Whatever it was, he'd missed having her around.

"So? You changed your mind about Wainwright? Decided not to get married after all?"

"Of course not. I've simply decided not to marry Wexford."

He chuckled. "I must say, I applaud your good sense. He's not the reliable type. Anybody who failed second grade is not reliable. You need somebody steady, somebody to keep you out of trouble."

"I'm not concerned one whit about his reliability. It was his ears."

"His ears?"

"Yes. They were too big. I discovered it right away."

"When you were wallowing in his lap?"

"I was not wallowing. I was seducing."

"Well, whatever you call it, it went a little too far for a first date."

"If you hadn't been skulking in the hallway, you never would have noticed."

"I wasn't skulking. I was being a polite host."

"Hah!"

He chuckled. "Maybe I was skulking. But I wasn't nearly as blatant as you that time you climbed the fig tree to spy on me and Mavalene Hunter."

"I was only fourteen."

"Yes, but you were sixteen when you put those frogs in June Hubbard's bathtub."

Joanna tipped back her head and roared with laughter. "I'll never forget the look on her face. She came flying out of the guest room, screaming bloody murder. Whatever happened to poor old June?"

"You very well know what happened to June. She broke our engagement that same weekend. I think she went on to marry somebody safe, a shoe salesman."

He watched in fascination as Joanna made one of her quick changes from laughter to seriousness.

"Why did Belinda leave you, Kirk?"

The question caught him off guard. The painful truth was that Belinda had divorced him because he was too old for her. He'd wanted nothing more than a contented wife, a house full of children, and the satisfaction of running Deerfield Manufacturing. Belinda had wanted more. No, had demanded more. First with cajolery, then later in a shrill voice and with temper tantrums. The more he'd tried to handle the situation, the worse it had gotten.

He had to admit that he'd failed miserably at his marriage, and he knew part of the fault was his. Belinda had often accused him of being too straitlaced and overbearing, and he suspected that Joanna might agree.

"Because I'm boring," he said.

"If she thought that, then she was a fool." Joanna put her glass on the table and looked at him. "How long has it been since you played basketball, Kirk?"

"Not since you left for college."

"I thought not. What you need, Kirk Maitland, is some fun in your life. Let's play a quick game of PIG."

"It's getting late. Aren't you ready for bed?"

"If you're trying to convince me that you're boring, you're not succeeding. I take that as plain lazy."

"And I take that as a challenge. You're on, Joanna Deerfield."

He was accustomed to a more sedate pace than Joanna set. He had to lengthen his stride to keep up with her. As they walked across the backyard, he noticed the smell of roses and jasmine and honeysuckle. He marveled at the brightness of the moon and the elegant beauty of the dark-shrouded trees. He couldn't remember the last time he'd taken the time to admire the beauty of nature.

"I'll get the ball." He had to speak around a big lump in his throat. As he ducked into the bathhouse and retrieved a basketball, he wondered how long it would be before some smart man took her offer and carried her to the altar. Then he wondered what in the hell he'd do if one did.

Kirk beat her soundly the first game.

"It's this wretched skirt," she said. Before he could protest, she unbuttoned it and tossed it across an oleander bush. Her blouse was long enough to cover everything except the lace on the bottom of her satin tap panties. Kirk knew what they were called because he remembered the first pair she'd ever bought. She'd been thirteen and had proudly lifted them from the box to show him her grown-up underwear.

But she was no longer thirteen, and the sight of her in blouse and satin panties had a most disturbing effect on him.

"What in the hell do you think you're doing?" He jerked the skirt off the bush and handed it back to her. "Put your clothes back on."

"It's not my clothes; it's just my skirt."

"I know what it is. Put it back on."

"Good grief, Kirk. You needn't act as if I'd stripped stark naked. This is a private court. Nobody can see me."

"*I* can see you, Joanna. Put the damned thing on."

She slung the skirt over her shoulder and glared at him. "If you think I'm going to put on this skirt because you order me to, you're sadly mistaken. I spent four years mincing around that convent, wearing a prissy little white blouse and a blue cotton skirt just because somebody decreed I should, listening to Bach and Beethoven when I wanted to hear Ray Charles and Linda Ronstadt, going to museums when I wanted to go to nightclubs."

"It was not a convent; it was a college."

"It was a prison. One you forced me to attend."

"You make me sound like a tyrant. I'm merely your guardian."

"You're a dictator. Well, I won't be dictated to anymore. Wexford didn't work out, but Clinton will."

"Who the hell is Clinton?"

"A man I saw this afternoon at the Minute Mart."

"You're bringing home somebody you've just met? And at the Minute Mart?"

Joanna could never stay angry long, especially at Kirk.

"Did anybody ever tell you that you look like a lovable old bear when you scowl?" She patted his face. "Actually, I didn't just meet him. He was on the Costa Brava two summers ago. We had some fun together." She reached up once more and patted his cheek. "Don't be an old grouch. You'll like him. He has friendly eyes."

"Clinton who? What does he do for a living?"

She waved her hand. "Oh, I think he's in stocks and bonds or something boring like that. I forget his last name—it's been such a long time since I've seen him. I couldn't very well ask a man to marry me and say, 'By the way, what's your last name?' I think it's Goober or Goodbar or Gable. Something like that."

He bit back a torrent of blue language that would have blistered her ears. "I feel six new gray hairs coming on."

"On you they look good." With her skirt still draped over her shoulder, she went toward the house, whistling a tune Kirk didn't know. No doubt some bawdy song she'd learned on the Costa Brava, he thought.

He stood on the basketball court and watched until he saw the light come on in Joanna's bedroom. She'd be safe now, in bed. At least he hoped she was going to bed. For all he knew she might be planning to slide down the cherry tree outside her window and go off to meet Goodbar or Goober or whatever the hell his name was.

"I was not cut out to be a chaperon," he muttered.

Goober was just as bad as Kirk thought he'd be. Joanna had dragged him home and was parading him at the dinner table. Kirk figured she'd done it deliberately to ruin his digestion.

"What did you say your line of work is, Mr. Goober?"

"Gable." The skinny, ill-at-ease man ran a bony finger around his collar. Stretching his neck like a peacock, he adjusted his Adam's apple. "I'm a high-tech consultant. You know, work on microfiche and that sort of thing."

"I like rainbow trout better," Joanna said. "They're much more interesting."

Kirk gave her a behave-yourself nudge under the table. She knew damned well the difference between microfiche and rainbow trout. What was she trying to do? Confuse the poor man so much he didn't know the altar from the front door?

"She loves to tease," Kirk said.

Poor Gable laughed. "I found that out on the Costa Brava. One night she wanted to dance and all the night-clubs were closed. She talked me into dancing right on the street."

Kirk speared his steak as if it needed killing before he ate it. "Just how late was that?"

"Pay him no attention, Clinton. I told you he'd be an old bear. He's not used to these modern ideas."

That sounded ominous to Kirk. He knew better than to ask, but curiosity overcame his common sense. "What modern ideas, Joanna?"

She gave him a Madonna smile. "About matrimony."

He glared at Joanna, but his voice was deceptively mild as he turned to Gable. "It's been two years since you've seen her, hasn't it?" He didn't wait for confirmation. "You were probably surprised by her invitation to dinner."

Gable looked like a fish that had just been hooked and was trying to make the most of it. "Her dinner invitation didn't surprise me as much as the other one."

Kirk shot Joanna another murderous look before turning his attention back to their guest. "What other one?"

"The one to, ah, marry her. She came right up to me in the Minute Mart and asked if I'd be interested in matrimony. Naturally I saw what a card she was."

Kirk said a silent prayer of thanks that the man hadn't taken Joanna seriously. His laugh of relief was genuine. "She's a comic, all right."

"I wasn't kidding," Joanna said. "I'm desperate to get married."

Gable was not amused. "Desperate, did you say?"

"Yes." Joanna looked demurely at her plate. "In the family way."

Kirk actually felt sorry for the man as he struggled to keep from bolting to the door. He guessed he was getting soft with old age. He didn't know he could want to kill a man and feel sorry for him at the same time.

"Behave yourself, Joanna," he whispered. Turning to Gable, he said, "She's just teasing. She's in perfect condition. Not a thing wrong with her." He figured he'd made her sound like a good used car. Served her right for being so all-fired stubborn. Glancing her way, he saw her struggling to keep from laughing.

"Have all my teeth and everything," she added.

"Well, now..." Gable fiddled with his fork and his collar and his dinner napkin. Finally he stood up. "It's been a lovely evening, and I hate to eat and run, but I do have pressing business. It simply can't wait. Lovely seeing you again, Joanna, and I wish you all the luck with your, er, quest for matrimony."

Joanna stood up. "Let me see you to the door." She patted Gable's arm and led him out of the room. Kirk saw the magic she worked on him. She went from addle-brained tease to charming, gracious hostess. He'd be willing to bet that by the time they got to the front door, Gable would be wondering why he'd thrown away his golden opportunity to marry her.

Scooting his chair back from the table, Kirk made his way to the kitchen. By the time Joanna joined him, he had a pan of chicken soup heating on the stove. It had been Grandfather Deerfield's remedy for everything from headache to heartache.

She walked over and peered into the pan. "Chicken soup?"

"Ulcers. You're giving me ulcers."

"Nonsense. It's all that sexual repression."

He wondered if she read minds.

"No. It's all the Wexfords and Goobers you keep dragging home. If you're so determined to get married, at least choose somebody with some class."

"Hah!"

"What does that mean?"

"It means, look who's talking. Here you are, thirty-five years old and heating soup for ulcers instead of romping in bed with some warm and willing sex partner."

"Romping around in bed? Is that what you did that summer you were in Paris?"

"Well, there was that time at . . ."

"I don't want to hear about it," he shouted.

"Tsk, tsk. It's all that sexual repression. It's made you crabby."

"I am not crabby!"

"Then why are you shouting?"

Kirk threw his hands into the air as his soup boiled over. "I swear, Joanna, you're going to drive me to drink."

"I think a shot of Jack Daniels would do you more good right now than warm soup." She began to rummage in the cabinets. "Do you still keep some? I could use a good healthy swig myself. Did you notice Goober's feet?"

"What about his feet?"

"They were too skinny. I can't abide a man with skinny feet."

Kirk threw back his head and roared. "God, Joanna. I don't know whether to murder you or to kiss you."

In one of her quicksilver changes, she turned serious. "Neither. Help me find a husband."

He bought time by pulling a dishcloth from a drawer and swabbing up the mess he'd made of the soup. And as he did so, he thought of all the friendly discussions he and Joanna had had in the kitchen at Meadowlane. They'd always been able to tell each other their most private thoughts. He was suddenly filled with nostalgia and a need to recapture that wonderful camaraderie of their youth. Her friendship was too precious ever to lose.

Putting down the cloth, he took her gently by the shoulders. "Joanna, when are you going to give up this ridiculous idea? You were mad at me when you said you were going to find a husband. You don't have to go through with it."

"I want to," she said softly.

He knew Joanna too well not to recognize the sincerity in her tone. He'd hoped she would eventually give up the ridiculous marriage scheme she'd hatched half in rebellion and half in teasing playfulness. Those hopes came crashing down.

"You're serious about this, aren't you?" He hoped she would say no, but he knew that hope, too, was futile. Once Joanna set her mind on something, she was as unchangeable as the land.

"Yes." Her dark eyes were wide with appeal as she looked at him. "It's the best way I know to get out of your hair and carry on with a life style of my own choosing."

"You don't have to get married in order to have money. I'll send you to Siberia and Marbella and any place else you want to go. I'll even hire somebody to go with you to look after you. I'd go myself if I could leave Deerfield Manufacturing."

"No," she said softly.

"No?"

"I've given this matter some serious thought, Kirk. I know this whole thing was born out of impulse, but I've decided I like the idea of getting married." Her eyes began to sparkle. "Love is nice, don't you think? Look at Uncle Kenneth and Aunt Sophie. They're happy as two larks. And Mom and Dad had a good marriage, too. And just think about the children! Think what fun it would be to show them the Alps and Pikes Peak and The Grand Canyon." She smiled at him. "If I wait till I'm thirty-five, I might be too old."

Kirk struggled for control, fought to keep from getting caught up in Joanna's dream. She'd always had the knack for making the ordinary seem special.

"Joanna, marriage isn't that simple. It's not something you just decide to do."

"I just didn't decide. I told you, I've given it some thought."

He saw that stubborn chin come up. "Don't get balky with me. This is too important. Please just listen to what I have to say."

"I'm listening."

He smiled. "Then please listen with a less ferocious look on your face. It scares the hell out of me."

She bared her teeth in the caricature of a smile. "There. Is that better?"

"It'll do." He reached out and took her hand. "You're young and inexperienced, Joanna."

"And you're some big expert? Kirk, using my age against me is not fair. You made your mistake. Give me a chance to make mine."

He tightened his hold. "Don't pull away. I admit my failure. But whether you like it or not, I am older and more experienced than you. You're viewing love and marriage through rose-colored glasses. And while it can be wonderful, it doesn't always work out that way. A good marriage takes commitment and compromise and sometimes hard work."

"Good grief. You make it sound as dull as a balance sheet at Deerfield Manufacturing. No wonder Belinda—" She stopped, horrified at what she'd been about to say. The raw pain was there on Kirk's face. "Oh, God, I'm sorry, Kirk." She put her free hand on his face and tried to gently rub away the tension. "I'm so sorry. Please, please, forgive me. I didn't mean what I was going to say. You're wonderful, and Belinda must have been crazy to leave you." Her hand patted and caressed and soothed as she talked.

Kirk pulled her into his arms and pressed her face against his shoulder. "It's all right, baby. None of it was your fault. None of it."

She rested her head on his chest for a long time, enjoying the familiar feeling of security. How easy it would be just to stay there and let Kirk make all the decisions. Too easy, she decided. And too safe.

She lifted her head and looked up at him. "I heard everything you said. It was all wise and sensible and smart. But it's your way, Kirk, not mine. I've made my decision. I *am* going to get married. And nothing you can do will stop me."

He held her at arm's length. "If you're that determined to go through with it, then let me help you find someone suitable."

"Someone suitable?" She rolled her eyes heavenward. "I see I came to the wrong person for help. No, thank you, Kirk. I'll find my own husband."

"Please, Joanna. You've been gone a long time. I know the young men of the city better than you do. No strings attached. Just one friend helping another."

Suddenly Joanna smiled. She could never deny a gesture made out of friendship. "Yes. I'll let you help. But promise me one thing."

"What?"

"Find somebody wonderful. I want my husband to be the most wonderful man in the whole world."

She'd been practicing that charm on him since she was a child. And he was bewitched. As always. From the habit of many years, he led Joanna to a chair and lifted her onto his lap. Instantly he realized his mistake. This was no child he was holding; Joanna was a woman, an alluring woman with soft hair, scented skin and sensuous curves. Fighting his normal male reaction, forcing himself to remember his responsibility to take care of her, he tucked her into the curve of his arm and smoothed back her curls. "If that's what you want, I'll try to get it for you." He knew he was being foolish and softhearted, but he had never been able to deny Joanna anything, especially when she smiled. "I'll try to find somebody suitable for you."

"Not suitable. Wonderful," she reminded him. "And without big ears and skinny feet."

He chuckled. "And don't forget the pistachio nuts." He wound a hand in her soft curls and hugged her tighter. "I'll do my part, but you'll have to do yours, too. Falling in love takes time."

"I don't have much time. Just think of all the remarkable things that are happening all over the world right now that I'm missing. I thought I might just get married first and fall in love later.''

"You can't catch a husband the way you do a calf. You can't rope him and drag him to the altar.''

She twisted to look up at him. "I have a confession to make, Kirk.''

"I'm listening.''

"Promise you won't laugh.''

"Have I ever laughed at you when you've confided in me?''

"No.''

He touched her hair once more. It curled intimately around his fingers, as soft and silky as a kiss. He spoke around a big frog in his throat. "I promise you, baby, I won't laugh this time.''

"Well, I haven't…'' She paused, her cheeks turning pink as she struggled with her admission. Taking a deep breath, she plunged ahead, talking quickly to get it over with. "I haven't had much experience dating. When I was in high school, most of the boys were scared off by my money. And in Spain, young ladies of breeding are put on pedestals. There's not much to learn about men up there. And I've certainly never tried to get married before. I don't know how it's done.''

"With finesse.'' He pressed his lips to her hair.

They were still for a long time, enjoying the closeness of two people who were cousins by fate and best friends by design. The hall clock that Grandfather Deerfield had brought over from England chimed the hour, and Rags passed through the kitchen on his way to the doggie door. He paused beside them to see if he could rouse any interest in his evening stroll, but after two minutes of being totally ignored, he wagged his tail and continued his ramble alone.

Finally Joanna stirred. She twisted around and cupped Kirk's face. "Since you're going to find me a husband, I might as well give you my specifications."

He chuckled. "Another list of don'ts?"

"No. A list of dos. I want a man who is tall, about like you. And gray eyes would be nice, too, if you can find them. I've always been partial to your gray eyes. Now, dark hair isn't an absolute necessity. I like blond men, especially in the summer when their hair bleaches out, but I wouldn't mind a man with hair that dips over his forehead." She paused to smooth back his dark hair. "Kind of like yours," she added.

Kirk cleared the lump out of his throat. "That's a tall order, Joanna."

"I'm not finished yet. I want somebody who is smart. They might not be as brilliant as you, but they have to at least know the difference between microfiche and rainbow trout."

They laughed together.

"Oh, and don't forget about basketball. If he can't play PIG, I don't want him." She smiled up at him as a new idea took hold. "He has to be a good sailor, too. Remember all those good times we had when Grandfather Deerfield took us sailing?"

Kirk looked off into space, remembering Joanna with the wind in her hair, suntanned legs planted apart to accommodate the roll of the sailboat, laughing. She'd always been laughing when they sailed. He had, too. Those had been wonderful, carefree days. He wondered how he'd gotten so far from those days, why he'd given up sailing altogether.

"I remember, Joanna. It seems so long ago."

"It seems like only yesterday to me, and I want to do it again. I'm *going* to do it again." Kirk smiled as she set her jaw at an unconsciously stubborn angle. "I'm going to marry a man who will sail with me." Her eyes sparkled as she smiled up at him. "Just think of all the grand places we can discover together on a sailboat."

Kirk envied the man who would discover those places with her. Selfishly he begrudged another man the joy of sailing with Joanna. With her lively imagination and her spontaneous sense of fun she used to make each jaunt on their boat a high adventure. What would it be like to sail with her now that she was a woman? His mind boggled at the possibilities. One of those grand places they'd discover together would surely be heaven.

He fought to tame his imagination, to put everything back into perspective. "Anything else?"

"One more thing."

"What's that?"

"He has to be a good hugger and a good laugher. Men who can laugh and hug are usually generous and kind-hearted and compassionate and loving. Do you think you can find a man like that for me?" She stood up and smiled at him.

Kirk was lost and he knew it. Joanna had been twisting him around her little finger since she was three years old, and she'd done it again. He figured if he ever lived through her quest for matrimony, he'd be ready for a retirement home.

"I'll find the right man for you even if I have to bribe and browbeat him all the way to the altar." He reached out and took her hand. "You have to promise me one thing."

"Anything except to become a lady."

He chuckled at the mischievous look she gave him. Sometimes Joanna was pure imp. "Don't marry any man unless you love him—no matter how anxious you are and how much he fits your specifications." He squeezed her hands. "Give yourself time to find love. Promise me, Jo-anna."

"I will if you will."

"Will what?"

"Find love."

"But I'm not looking for love, Joanna."

"Maybe you don't have to look; maybe love will find you." She leaned over and tenderly kissed his jaw.

"Good night, Kirk."

He was thoughtful as he watched her leave. Switching off the kitchen light, he stood in the darkness for a while, trying to sort everything out. He'd never seen a problem that couldn't be worked out with careful analysis and de-cisive action. But this business with Joanna defied analy-sis. He was working with so many unknowns he felt like a blind man.

"Make that a blind fool," he amended, "an *old* blind fool." He left the kitchen and went into his study to work. He always turned to work when he was disturbed. And there was no doubt about it, the prospect of finding Jo-anna a husband disturbed him. "Besides that, she has me talking to myself."

He shut himself up in his study, pulled out his file on the proposed acquisition of Granlan Company and set to work.

Upstairs, Joanna leaned against her bedroom door, lis-tening for the sounds of Kirk's footsteps on the stairs. Af-ter five minutes, when there were none, she opened her door a crack and peered into the hallway. It was empty. Kirk was probably in his study working. He worked much too hard, she thought. She felt a twinge of guilt. If she'd come home during vacations instead of traveling all over Europe, maybe she could have prevented him from be-coming a workaholic.

She started to go downstairs to engage him in a game of chess, but changed her mind. Instead she leaned against the door, mulling over her present situation. Hadn't she disrupted Kirk's life enough already, dragging him out to play ball when he didn't want to, enlisting his help in finding a husband?

The last thought made her shiver. What had she gotten herself into? Her experience with men had been limited to a few flirtations and some harmless kissing. Goose bumps popped up on her arms as she realized she hadn't really turned down Wexford and Clinton because of big feet and skinny ears or a penchant for pistachios. True, she didn't like any of those things. But the fact was, she was scared.

She felt a great longing to run downstairs and seek the shelter of Kirk's arms. And that scared her, too. Life outside the convent walls was so complicated.

"Hellfire and damnation, Joanna. You're moping." Saying the words that Kirk had declared off limits made her feel better. She walked across the room and kicked the bed. The defiant gesture restored her spirits even more. She browsed through the bookshelf above her desk until she found a good bawdy book, one the nuns would never have allowed her to read.

Then she settled down to a few hours of forbidden pleasure.

Chapter Three

Kirk wasted no time in finding the right man for Joanna, figuring that if he didn't act quickly she'd run out and drag home another sorry specimen who had failed second grade, or worse. He knew how stubborn she was. Once she'd set her mind to marrying, nothing would stop her. The only control he could exercise would be over her choice of a bridegroom. Maybe he could prevent her from ruining her life by selecting a sensible young man who would watch out for her.

The day after their talk in the kitchen, he heard the sound of music. Loud music. Following the sound, he found Joanna in the parlor, dressed in a costume so blatantly sexy it would sober skid-row bums. Head thrown back, arms uplifted, she was dancing to the music, blissfully unaware of her audience.

Kirk stood in the doorway, spellbound. He recognized the costume and the music as Spanish. He didn't know what the dance was called, but it had obviously been designed to make fools of men like him. The sensuous beat of the music and the graceful undulation of Joanna's hips ripped through his gut like a knife. Making a strangled sound, he turned from the doorway to leave.

"Going somewhere, Kirk?"

He whirled back around. Joanna was standing so close he could see a fine sheen of perspiration across the tops of her breasts.

"Do you always go around dressed like that?"

She stepped back, eyes blazing. "This happens to be an authentic flamenco dress."

"I can see your navel and your..." Words failed him.

"Do you expect me to dance in a shroud? The flamenco calls for a dress that's bright and sassy."

"It's indecent."

"Indecent?" Her voice was deceptively soft as she stepped back from him. "You want to see indecent?" Reaching up, she grabbed the masses of ruffles on her shoulders and slid them down her arms. The move not only exposed a heady expanse of tanned shoulders, it further bared her breasts.

Propping her hands on her hips, Joanna defied him. "How's that for indecent, Kirk?"

He gripped her shoulders and glared down at her. Suddenly everything about her overwhelmed him—the bare shoulders, sweat slick and sexy, the soft mounds of her breasts, swelled in heady invitation above the outrageous gown, the lips, berry ripe and parted. He knew he was out of control, but it didn't seem to matter anymore.

His mouth crushed down on hers. He was avidly aware of its texture, soft and moist and velvety. The shape of her lips burned into his memory, full and sensuous and openly inviting. Before he could stop himself, he was kissing her with undisguised passion.

He felt her wild response, felt her nipples harden and peak against his shirt, felt her hips shift to fit perfectly against his.

With a muttered oath he jerked his head up. Still gripping her arms, he looked down at her.

"That's what happens to innocent girls who flaunt themselves."

Joanna felt as if she had suddenly been caught in a whirlwind. She was angry and elated and confused, all at the same time. Her only satisfaction was that Kirk didn't seem to be his usual cool self. There was a decided huskiness in his voice.

"I'm a woman, Kirk. And don't you forget that." She was surprised at the calmness in her own voice.

He didn't say anything, merely looked at her with those turbulent gray eyes. In the screaming silence of the room, she faced him. Time marched by in storm-trooper boots, and each passing minute jolted her nerves. But she remained staunch. She knew that battles weren't won by timidity.

Finally Kirk loosened his grip. "I'm sorry, Joanna. I didn't mean to do that."

"Most men who kiss me don't apologize afterward."

"It wasn't a kiss; it was..."

"Was what?"

"A lesson. I wanted to show you how easy it is to provoke a man to..."

"To what?"

"To that kind of behavior. You have to be careful, Joanna."

He removed his hands from her shoulders, and his expression became contrite. Reaching out, he gently rubbed her shoulders. "I'm so sorry, baby. Did I hurt you?"

She looked down at the faint imprint of his fingers on her skin. "No, Kirk. You may be trying to turn me into a porcelain doll, but I'm not fragile."

Kirk walked away from her and sat on the sofa. "Would you mind turning down that music, Joanna? I have something important to tell you."

"Does the music bother you?"

"Immensely."

"Then I'll turn it off. I've finished dancing, anyhow." After she'd flipped the switch on the tape player, she sat down in a chair opposite him.

"I've found a young man for you."

The news didn't cheer her at all. "A husband?"

"Merely a prospect. His name is Alfred Oakland. He's a sharp young man, one of the CPAs in our accounting department at Deerfield Manufacturing. I've arranged a double date for tonight."

That news cheered her even less. She'd be damned if she'd ask who his date was. "That sounds absolutely lovely." She smiled at him.

For a minute he just sat on the sofa, watching her. Then he said, "Dinner at eight."

"Great." She stood up. "I have to go upstairs and make myself ruinously gorgeous."

As it turned out, Kirk's date was someone Joanna knew, Marsha Holmes. Marsha was a cool blonde, sophisticated, understated and successful. She had her own law practice, was president of the League of Women Voters and was so polished she squeaked when she walked.

Joanna hated her. She tried hard not to. As she watched the two of them across the dinner table, she tried to be happy that Kirk had found someone so suitable. But did she have to be so damned beautiful, too? Joanna fumed.

No wonder Kirk was so taken with her, bending over to catch her every word, sitting so close Joanna just knew their knees were touching under the table.

She tried to concentrate on her own date, but her heart wasn't in it. The memory of being in Kirk's arms this afternoon coursed through her like new wine. She didn't know how it had happened nor why, but that kiss had almost made her forget her plans.

Resolutely she turned to her own companion.

"Tell me all about your job, Alfred."

Alfred launched into a lengthy monologue about balance sheets and tax forms and debits and credits. Joanna tried hard to concentrate, but her mind kept wandering toward Kirk. She wondered what Marsha had said to make his beautiful mouth curve upward in a smile. She had a sudden, intense urge to dump her blackened redfish into Marsha's lap. With a shock Joanna realized that she was jealous. It was a new emotion for her, and she sat back, feeling suddenly contrite. What was happening to her?

Before she turned back to Alfred, Joanna peeked across the table just in time to see Marsha reach up and tenderly touch Kirk's cheek. He caught Joanna staring and smiled.

"Joanna, you're not eating your fish. I'm surprised. Your appetite's usually so hardy."

"Ulcers," she said.

Kirk couldn't suppress his grin. "It must be the climate."

"No doubt. Too much hot air."

Marsha was not to be left out of the conversation. "Mississippi is unusually sultry this summer."

"Tupelo in particular," Alfred added.

"Meadowlane is practically steaming." Kirk was looking directly into Joanna's eyes when he spoke.

"Especially the parlor." She could feel the searing heat of his gaze before he slowly turned back to his companion. The warmth seemed to seep through her skin and creep slowly through her body. She wondered if anybody had ever been ravished in the glassed-in dining room at Gloster 205, the fanciest restaurant in town. One more look like that from Kirk and she could be across the table having her way with him, right in plain sight of all the Friday night diners and everybody who was headed through the Crosstown intersection for the second feature at the movies.

That was a hell of a way to think about the man she'd always thought of as her cousin and her best friend.

To Alfred, she said gaily, "I have a sudden urge to dance."

"That sounds lovely," Marsha said. "Bogart's would be nice."

"Does that suit everybody?" Kirk asked.

Joanna didn't even want to be breathing the same air as Marsha. She was afraid of committing murder with a half-eaten fish. And as for Kirk—if she didn't get away from him, she would probably do something they'd both regret.

"You two go ahead." Joanna dismissed them with a wave of her hand. "I want to dance on the street." Linking her arm with Alfred's, she smiled up at him. "Is that all right with you?"

Alfred knew he couldn't say no, even to such an outrageous proposition, for he had long ago become a victim to Joanna's smile. "We might try the park," he said mildly.

"Great." Holding Alfred's arm, Joanna swept by Kirk without glancing his way. "Look for me when you see me coming," she called over her shoulder.

"Joanna," Kirk called after her. But she never even looked back.

Alfred and Joanna ended up at Joyner Park, and with Joanna humming the tunes and sometimes teaching him the steps, they danced until he begged for relief.

"I can think of better ways to die." He was panting and laughing as they sat down on the merry-go-round.

"So can I. And all of them are wicked."

"You're delightful, Joanna. I'm glad Kirk talked me into coming."

"He can be a fierce old bear when he wants to. Did he use bribery or force?"

Alfred gave her an appreciative look. "More like a command. To tell the truth, when one is asked to date the boss's cousin, it's usually best to go prepared with a muzzle and a chain."

Joanna impulsively hugged him. "You're honest and forthright. I like that, Alfred. I think we're going to be good friends."

"I was hoping for more than that."

Joanna stepped off the merry-go-round and began to pace. "This is all very complicated, Alfred." She tilted her face toward the sky and studied the stars for a moment. "I thought I was hoping for more than that, too. As a matter of fact, I'd planned to marry you."

He laughed. "Do you mind if we wait until you've learned my last name?" She turned to stare at him. "It's Oakland. You've called me Kirkland all night."

"I'm sorry."

"You're forgiven. But that forgiveness comes with a price. Do you mind telling me *why* you had planned to marry me? I'd love to think it's my irresistible charm, but even I'm not that big a fool."

"I suppose I owe you the truth since, in a way, I've used you. You see, Kirk isn't really my cousin; he's my guardian. He controls my inheritance until I'm thirty—or married. So I devised a scheme to get married and gain my independence. All very logical and practical."

"Yes. But not romantic."

She smiled at him in appreciation. "You're a very perceptive man. My scheme was impulsive, to say the least. I'm beginning to think it was harebrained, as well. Don't get me wrong. You're exceptionally nice and I'm no expert on love or anything, but I wonder if it shouldn't feel—well, less practical."

"Hearts and flowers and violins?"

She laughed. "Yes. And balloons and bazookas and confetti. I want love to feel like a celebration."

"I suspect that being in love with you would be a celebration." He took her hand. "Joanna, I want to take you out again."

"But just as friends, Alfred, okay? I don't think I can go on with this husband-hunting scheme, and I certainly don't want to mislead you. You're too nice."

"Friends, Joanna. But don't count me out, yet. Many a fine romance has started with a beautiful friendship."

She gave him one last appreciative look, then lifted her gaze to the stars.

"Wishing on a star? I used to do that when I was young. Believed in it, too. What did you wish for, Joanna?"

She closed her eyes to shut out the star shine, but the brightness was still there. She sighed softly as she realized she was envisioning the brightness of her future. "Love," she said with her eyes still shut. "I wish for love."

* * *

Joanna got home at two o'clock in the morning, early
for her. As she passed Kirk's bedroom she noticed that his
door was open. She stuck her head around the corner.

"Kirk?"

There was no reply. In the dimness of the bedside lamp,
she could see that his bed hadn't been slept in.

"Still out with that hussy," she muttered.

She stomped down the hall to her bedroom, started to
strip off her dress, then changed her mind. "Lord knows
what time he'll come in," she added as she marched down
the stairs. "Probably dragging that brazen baggage with
him. 'Unusually sultry in Mississippi,' indeed! The way she
was acting over him ought to be outlawed. I ought to hire
a good lawyer and sue!"

Rags jumped up from his resting place near the bottom
of the stairs, startled awake by Joanna's tirade. He followed her into the kitchen, tucking his tail between his legs
as she loudly banged cabinet doors.

"Where does he keep the Jack Daniels?" Joanna demanded, glaring down at the small dog.

Rags put his head on the floor and covered his eyes with
his paws. "Even Rags is ashamed of the way he carried on
over that floozy," Joanna assured herself just as she discovered the bourbon in one of the lower cupboards. She
poured herself a generous shot and took a big gulp. It
burned all the way to her stomach. She took another big
slug and refilled her glass. "Cheers, Rags. Here's to me
and you and this lonesome big house." She headed toward the kitchen table with her glass, then changed her
mind. "If I'm going to be maudlin, I might as well be
drunk, too."

Taking the bottle with her, she moved to the table and
sat down. For a while there was no sound in the kitchen

except the splash of whiskey into the glass and an occasional dramatic sigh from Joanna.

"Helluva thing about love. It creeps up on you, even when you don't want it to." She propped her face on her hands and stared morosely into her glass. "Now you take strangers. It's so easy. Like falling into a needle in a haystack." She spaced the words carefully, pronouncing each in a sonorous voice. "Take bes' frien's, for instance. Then it gets complicated. Like teaching new dogs old tricks."

"Joanna?"

She turned her head slightly, quirked an eyebrow and leered at Kirk, standing in the doorway.

"Can't teach new dogs," she intoned.

"I do believe you're sloshed."

"Tell it to her honor, the blond law hussy."

Kirk grinned. "Didn't anybody ever tell you that you shouldn't drink alone?"

"My bes' frien'. A jillion times."

He crossed to her and gently took the glass from her hand. Carefully he assessed her condition and the level of liquor in the bottle. "You're going to have the devil of a hangover tomorrow." Putting his arms around her shoulders, he half lifted her from the chair. "Can you stand?"

"I stand on principles." Her legs wobbled as she peered owlishly up at him.

Chuckling, Kirk scooped her into his arms.

"Feels wunnerful." She snuggled her head against his chest.

"Yes, it does, baby."

She shut one eye and squinted up at him. "I'm not a baby. I'm all woman."

"So I've noticed."

"W-O-M-M-A-N."

"Jack Daniels has improved your spelling, I see."

Kirk switched off the light with his shoulder and carried her from the kitchen. She snuggled against his chest and began to nibble his throat.

"You taste good. Like a bes' frien' should." She gave a deep throaty chuckle and smiled up at him.

He almost forgot she was drunk. Desire flared through him, ignited by the feel of her in his arms and fanned by the moist touch of her mouth against his skin.

"I'm going to tuck you into bed, Joanna." He walked with purpose toward the stairs.

"Sounds wunnerful." She unfastened the two top buttons on his shirt and carefully flicked her tongue across his chest. "Yummy."

"Joanna. Don't do that."

"I want to gobble you up."

Standing at the foot of the stairs, he gazed down at her. "Tomorrow we'd both regret it."

"We use' to pretend. Let's pretend there's no tomorrow." She popped open another button and spread her palm against his chest. "I feel your heart."

"Behave, Joanna." He removed her hand, and as he did he noticed her face, flushed with desire. "Lord, help me remember my responsibility." His words were half groan, half mutter.

"Wha'sat?"

"Nothing, Joanna."

He tore his gaze away from her and started up the steps. Her hand moved back to his chest and began a small, erotic circling. As he fought against his desire, each step he took became an agony for him. Joanna pushed aside his shirt and wet his nipple with a kiss. Ignoring the flames that shot through him, Kirk continued resolutely up the stairs.

Chapter Four

Kirk pushed open the door to Joanna's bedroom. It smelled of jasmine, sweet and heady and subtly seductive. The fragrance assaulted his senses, attacked his already ragged nerves.

Moonlight spilled through the windows and silvered a section of the bed covers. A black nightgown lay in its path. Kirk made a strangled sound as a vision of Joanna in that sultry wisp of satin and lace came to his mind. He hurried toward the bed, knowing that the quicker he got out of her bedroom, the better off they'd both be.

Leaning down, he placed Joanna tenderly on top of the covers. She kept her arms locked tightly around his neck. He would have fallen on top of her if he hadn't braced himself with his hands.

"Let go, Joanna, so I can tuck you in."

"No." She pulled harder so that his face was only inches from hers. "You look wunnerful in the dark. Jus' wunnerful."

"You do, too, baby. Now let go."

She held him fast. "Betcha didn't call ol' Marsha a baby."

Supporting his weight with his left arm, he tried to pry Joanna's fingers off his neck. "We'll talk about this tomorrow."

"Betcha kissed her. Show me how you kissed her, Kirk."

Looking down at her with the moonlight caught in her bright hair and shining on her beautiful innocent face, he struggled with temptation. The desire to kiss her was so strong he could almost taste it.

"You don't know what you're asking."

Finally he succeeded in getting her hands loose. He got off the bed so fast, Joanna bounced as the bedsprings released his weight. Before he could move away, she sat up and circled her arms around his hips.

"Don't go. I'll be sad and lonesome and blue."

She pressed her face against his abdomen and sighed. He clenched his jaw and tried to remain cool and collected, but that last move of hers had put the situation almost beyond his control. His hands were rough as he untangled her and pushed her back onto the bed.

"Behave yourself, Joanna."

"Tha's mean, Kirk. Don't be a meanie."

He knelt beside the bed and took her face between his hands. "I'm sorry, baby. I didn't intend to be rough with you. But you have to remember that I'm only human. I know you're too drunk to understand any of this, but I feel compelled to say it. You're a beautiful, desirable woman, and tonight you've exasperated me . . ." He paused and gazed into her face, then he added softly, "And tempted me almost beyond endurance." He tenderly brushed her hair back from her forehead, then cupped her face again. "Do you understand any of this, sweetheart?"

She gave him a crooked smile. "Do sweethearts kiss? Teach me."

"Ah, Joanna. You tempt me so. What am I going to do about you?" He closed his eyes and fought to regain control. The effort was great, but he finally managed to fight down his desire and steady his breathing.

Releasing her, he stood up—slowly, like an old man. She was smiling sleepily at him, looking innocent and young, so very young.

"Let's just hope that you don't remember any of this in the morning and that I have the courage to forget it."

Joanna mumbled something unintelligible and tried to keep her eyes open. The Jack Daniels had finally caught up with her.

With a sigh of relief Kirk sat on the edge of the bed and removed her high-heeled sandals. "No stockings, Joanna? I wonder if Alfred noticed." Her feet were small and tanned and unexpectedly sexy. He was thoughtful as he held that warm flesh in his hands. Then he bent over and tenderly kissed each toe.

Behind him, Joanna heaved one last sigh as she slipped into sleep. Kirk turned around and studied her. She was sleeping with both arms thrown back, hands open, palms up, yellow sundress billowing around her like a buttercup. The moonlight slanted across one bare arm so that he could see her pulse beating there. Her vulnerability clutched at his heart. Never had the burden of responsibility felt so heavy.

He knew her dress would become restricting and uncomfortable, but removing it was beyond his capabilities. He might be a martyr, he thought, but he was not a fool. There was no way he could bare that beautiful body and keep his nobility, let alone his sanity. He settled for bending down and unfastening her belt. Then he took an afghan off a nearby rocker and covered her.

He was tempted to lean down and kiss her forehead. It had always been the natural thing to do. Four years ago he would have thought nothing about it. But tonight, just that simple act seemed foolhardy.

"Goodnight, Joanna." He turned swiftly and left the room before he could change his mind.

Sunshine and bird song poured through Joanna's window. She sat up in bed and clutched her head. "When did birds stop singing and take up screeching? Ohh, my head." She noticed that she was fully dressed and covered by an afghan. That meant Kirk had put her to bed. But she didn't have any extra energy to expend on worrying over that matter. Every bone in her body seemed to be screaming in sympathy with her head, and her mouth tasted like feathers.

She eased back the covers, being careful not to make any unnecessary moves, and crept across the room. Before she reached the bathroom, she decided Kirk had moved it to China. Her hands were shaky on the water faucet, but she managed to splash her face and brush her teeth. She even slipped off her wrinkled dress and got into the blue terrycloth robe hanging on the bathroom hook. Just when she thought she was on the way to recovery, somebody took a sledgehammer and battered on her door. At least that's what it sounded like, she decided, as she clutched her throbbing temples.

"Coming," she muttered.

Rose was standing in the doorway with a tray of steaming food, every inch the proper housekeeper. Her white cap and apron were stiff with starch, and her smile was stiff with propriety. Although she'd been serving the Deerfields for twelve years, she always maintained a courteous and professional distance. Joanna knew that Rose would maintain that proper manner even if a herd of goats stampeded through the house. Nonetheless, she greeted the old housekeeper in her usual manner, with a hug.

Only the flush on Rose's cheeks betrayed her pleasure. "Mr. Kirk said I should serve you in bed."

"I can't eat a thing. Please take it away."

"Mr. Kirk's orders. He's worried because you missed breakfast and lunch. Told me to bring this food up and make sure you ate."

"He did, did he?" Unconsciously Joanna assumed her rebel's pose, chin stuck out, dark eyes gleaming, feet planted wide apart. She was absolutely furious that Kirk extended his authority even over her meals. Her fury was stoked by memories of the way Marsha Holmes had hung over him last night. "And where is my guardian?" She made the question deceptively soft and innocent. Her mind was already spinning with defiant plots, and she didn't want to arouse Rose's suspicions.

"Downstairs in his study. Working."

"Poor sweet old thing. And on Saturday, too." Joanna waved her hand toward the bedside table. "Just put the tray over there, Rose, then you can go. I know you have more important things to do than pamper me."

The dishes rattled as Rose set the tray down. "I don't like to leave until I see you eating. You know Mr. Kirk. He's a stickler for detail. He'll probably check the tray to see how much you ate."

He probably would, Joanna thought, and she didn't want to cause trouble for Rose. She lifted the cover off her plate and picked up a hot croissant. Bravely she took a small bite, then smiled at Rose. "It's delicious. Thank you.

I didn't know I was so hungry." Swallowing back a grimace, she took another bite.

"That's a good girl. I'll come back later for the empty tray."

"That won't be necessary." Joanna gave Rose her brightest smile. The effort made her feel as if her whole face would crack. She'd never known that a hangover could make your skin hurt. "Since Kirk was so thoughtful, I'll take the tray down and thank him in person."

"That should please him."

Joanna grinned. "It might even astonish him." She took Rose's arm and escorted her out the door. "Thank you again for the food."

As soon as the door was closed, she took several deep breaths. Getting oxygen to her brain restored her considerably. Thoughts of her confrontation with Kirk restored her even more. Taking the tray with her, she walked to the window and opened the sash.

"Come here, birdies, you loudmouthed little devils. Here's something for you to sing about." She crushed the croissants and flung the crumbs out the window. Activity was beginning to make her feel almost human again. The tomato juice on her tray looked good, and she was beginning to be hungry, but she'd be darned if she'd eat simply because Kirk ordered her to. Resolutely she poured her tomato juice down the toilet and flushed it through.

Then she dressed in jeans and sneakers, fluffed a brush through her hair and tiptoed downstairs, breakfast tray in hand. She found Rags in the downstairs hallway, sleeping near the bookcase. It didn't take much coaxing to get him interested in egg-and-ham soufflé. He followed her outside, his tail wagging.

After Joanna had done all her dastardly deeds, she walked triumphantly into Kirk's study, carrying the empty dishes. He looked up from his desk and smiled, but she was determined not to be sidetracked by the way his eyes crinkled at the corners and the way that lock of hair dipped down across his forehead.

"Hello, Joanna. You look beautiful today. Fresh and full of vitality." His voice did funny things to her, too. Words failed her. Suddenly she could do nothing except stare at him, excessively pleased by the compliment. She wondered if he'd said the same lovely things to Marsha. The thought made her extremely jealous, and a little uncomfortable. She vaguely remembered discussing Marsha with him last night. Her only hope was that, in spite of the whiskey, she'd maintained a certain amount of aloof dignity.

Kirk stared at her so long, she felt like fidgeting, but she remained staunch. Being at a loss for words was bad enough; she certainly wouldn't show her discomfort by fidgeting. His gray eyes continued to search hers. He seemed to be probing her mind, trying to read her thoughts. His stare completely mesmerized her. She couldn't have spoken if her life had depended on it. She was relieved when he finally broke the silence.

"How are you feeling today, Joanna?"

"Well enough to take care of myself, thank you very much." With elaborate politeness, she placed the tray with its empty dishes on his desk.

"Good. You ate. And I see the roses are back in your cheeks. Food is just what you needed."

"And you always know exactly what I need. Is that right, Kirk? For your information, I gave the food to Rags and the birds. I flushed the juice down the toilet."

She saw his smile fade and his eyes darken with wariness. "If you came here looking for battle, Joanna, you came to the right place." He stood up, towering over her.

She jerked her head up and looked him squarely in the eye, refusing to be intimidated. "Now that you've recovered from your hangover, I have a few words to say to you. Don't you know better than to get sloshed alone? You might have fallen down the staircase." He reached out and gripped her shoulders. "You were completely vulnerable. What if I hadn't been the one to walk in on you? Something terrible could have happened to you."

"A lot you cared. It was two o'clock in the morning when I came home. You were still out with that—that lawyer creature."

"I left you with a nice, responsible young man. Why couldn't you come home and go to bed like an ordinary woman?"

"Alfred was too shy to do that on our first date."

Kirk muttered an oath that would have made any other woman shake in her sneakers. Joanna merely glared at his tight jaw and the white line of anger around his mouth.

"Dammit, Joanna, if I ever find Alfred in your bed—or any other man for that matter—I swear to God I'll kill him." The intensity of his statement shocked Kirk as much as it did Joanna. For a moment they merely stared at each other. Struggling to make a rapid recovery, Kirk amended his rash statement. "You're so all-fired determined to rush right to the altar, I'm surprised I didn't find Alfred trussed up and waiting like a turkey."

"Well, *you're* the one who introduced him to me."

"I take it the match didn't work out."

"You needn't look so pleased. As a matter of fact, I like Alfred."

"Good. I'm glad."

"Then why are you scowling?"

"I'm not scowling. I have a bug in my eye."

"Bend over and let me see." She reached for him. As soon as she touched him, all her frustration vanished. She no longer felt the need to defy him, merely the need to touch him. With her hand on his face, she marveled at the strange power he seemed to hold over her.

Kirk jerked his head back and abruptly released his hold on her shoulders.

"Don't... Thank you, Joanna, but I don't need any help."

"Neither do I, Kirk." At her soft tone of voice, she saw his expression change, saw the tension leave. And she was glad. She didn't know why. All she knew was that she didn't want to fight with him anymore, didn't want to add to his stress. She glanced at his cluttered desk. Any man who brought home work on Saturday surely must be carrying a big burden of responsibility. It suddenly occurred to her that she might actually be able to lighten his load.

Kirk sighed and ran a hand wearily over his face. "I'm sorry we fought, baby. We seem to be doing a lot of that lately."

"I'm sorry, too. It's my fault, Kirk. Everybody used to say that I was a handful, even Grandfather Deerfield. I guess I always feel compelled to live down to that reputation."

"You're fine, Joanna. There's nothing wrong with you." He moved around behind his desk and sat down. If Joanna hadn't known better, she would have called it a retreat.

She perched on the edge of the desk and crossed her legs. Kirk suddenly gripped the desktop as if it were his last refuge. Joanna glanced from his hands to his face. The strain was showing again. Dear Kirk, she thought.

"I've decided it's time for me to take more responsibility. Especially since I'm planning to be married."

"I'm listening."

"I can't flit around the world forever. Sometime I'm going to have to settle down and become a productive citizen."

"That sounds like a good idea. What do you have in mind? An art career?"

"No. Bright and early Monday morning I'm starting work at Deerfield Manufacturing."

"Because of Alfred?"

Joanna's reasons were so complicated that even she didn't completely understand them. She knew she wanted to ease Kirk's work load, perhaps give him free time to enjoy life. She also knew that seeing him every day in his office would give her great satisfaction. She recognized that he was a man of brilliance and power, and she was proud of him. No, she thought, Alfred had nothing to do with her decision; but she wasn't sure that telling Kirk would be a good idea. Knowledge meant power and power meant control. For one of the few times in her life, Joanna exercised caution.

"You could say that."

"Then he's the one?"

"I plan to see him again. Yes. And I'm calling off the husband hunt."

"That's a relief."

Joanna thought he sounded about as relieved as a honey bear caught robbing the beehive. She hopped off the desk and hugged him.

"In spite of your growl, you're an old sweetie. Did you know that?" She added a kiss on the cheek to her cuddling. "Since I'm coming to work Monday, why don't you take the rest of the afternoon off and play golf?"

"I hate golf."

"Or tennis."

He removed her arms. "I have work to do, Joanna."

"It's a shame that you never have time for anything except work. But I suppose that's your way. I think I'll call Alfred and invite him over for a swim."

"Excellent."

Kirk opened a file folder and picked up a pencil. As the door banged shut behind Joanna, the pencil snapped in his hand. He threw the two halves viciously into the garbage can and sat staring at them. He knew he should be feeling grateful that Joanna had settled on a nice young man like Alfred—a man *he* had picked out for her. Furthermore, he should be thanking his lucky stars that she didn't seem to remember anything that had happened last night—not the way she'd kissed his chest nor the way he'd confessed his temptation. But he felt neither relief nor gratitude. What he felt was a frustration so explosive he wanted to take it out on something. Or somebody. Maybe even Alfred. Alfred, who would be at his house as soon as Joanna called him. Seeing the two of them together had all the appeal of sticking splinters under his fingernails. He wasn't going to sit around and watch it.

With a muttered curse Kirk slammed his file folder shut and walked toward the door. If Joanna could come to Deerfield Manufacturing, he could go to that damned country club and take up golfing. Even if it killed him.

Kirk stayed on the golf course until dark, hoping he had missed Alfred's swim at Deerfield.

The first thing he saw when he arrived home was Alfred's car. He went in the front door with all the anticipation of the Christians facing the lions. Sounds of music came from the parlor. He didn't know anything about music, but he would swear that particular song had been designed for seduction. It had a slow, bluesy timbre and a slow, pulsing beat. He had intended to walk on by, as if he were any sane adult, but as he passed the open doorway he saw Joanna in Alfred's arms. He paused, not meaning to stare. But he couldn't help himself. Alfred had Joanna pressed so close a slivered almond wouldn't fit between them. Furthermore, his left hand was resting on her hip. If what they were doing was called dancing, Kirk decided they needed a chaperon.

Kirk went into the parlor and leaned casually against the back of the sofa. The dancers hadn't even noticed him.

"Nice music," he said, loud enough that they could hear him.

They greeted him and kept on dancing. They didn't even have the decency to move apart. Seeing them up close was even worse than viewing them from the doorway. Their hips looked as if they'd been glued together. He felt a sudden urge to rip Joanna out of Alfred's arms and toss him out the door.

Controlling his temper, he rammed his balled fists into his pockets.

"What's that dance called?" He thought he'd spoken in a nice conversational tone, but the way Alfred jumped, he must have let his anger slip through.

"It doesn't really have a name," Alfred said. "It's just moving to the music."

Kirk thought they could have stood farther apart to do that, but he didn't say so. He was proud of his restraint. He stood behind the sofa, and the music pulsed on. He wondered if the infernal song would ever end.

Finally Alfred released Joanna. Kirk didn't know he'd been so tense until he felt his whole body relax.

"Thanks for having me over, Joanna. It's been a real pleasure," Alfred said, extending his hand.

"You're not leaving? I thought we were going to get take-out Chinese food and make an evening of it."

Alfred glanced Kirk's way. "I don't want to intrude."

Kirk smiled. "Don't mind me."

Turning back to Joanna, Alfred took her hand. "Would you give me a rain check?"

"Certainly."

"Joanna, I'm glad you'll be at Deerfield. I look forward to helping you get adjusted."

"Thanks, Alfred."

Joanna took his arm and escorted him to the door. Inside the parlor, the music stopped playing. Kirk listened to the sound of their footsteps, noting that there was hardly a pause long enough for any serious kissing. He took a perverse satisfaction in the knowledge. When Joanna came back into the parlor, he was actually grinning.

"Did you two have a nice afternoon, Joanna?"

"Is that a nosy question or a brotherly one?"

"Does it matter?"

"Yes. I don't answer nosy questions."

"The inquiry is motivated strictly out of concern for your well-being."

"In that case—yes, we had a lovely afternoon. Where did you disappear to?" She crossed the room and sat down beside him, so close he caught a whiff of her perfume. Jasmine. The heady fragrance brought back memories of last night. An unexpected surge of desire coursed through him.

He got off the sofa and began to prowl around the room. "I went golfing."

"Golfing? I thought you hated golf."

"I did. I still do. It was every bit as bad as I had expected. The sun cooked my head and I think I got calluses from so much walking. Nobody in his right mind would want to chase plastic balls into puny holes all day long.''

When Joanna laughed, she threw back her head, baring her throat and setting her red curls aswing. Kirk wondered what it would be like to press his lips against the base of that delicate throat.

''Have you decided to take up a hobby, Kirk?''

''Maybe.''

''I'm glad. You work too hard. You need something to balance your life.''

''It damned sure won't be golf.''

''How about dancing?''

''I'm afraid I'm as inept on the dance floor as I am on the golf course.''

''Dancing is just moving to the rhythm.''

''I have no rhythm.''

''Surely you danced when you were...''

''Young?''

''I wasn't going to say that. I was going to say, in school.''

''No. Of course, I went to a few, but I never seemed to get the hang of it. Besides, dancing was not high on my list of priorities.''

''I'll teach you.''

Before he could protest, Joanna had taken him by the hand and dragged him toward the stereo system. She rammed a new tape into the deck, and the room was once again filled with sultry music. When she moved into his arms he discovered that holding her close was as natural as breathing.

She smiled up at him. ''For slow dancing, the key is being able to feel the partner's rhythm. Like this.'' She pressed closer to him so that he could feel the shape of her thighs, the fullness of her breasts.

Kirk attempted to restrain his reaction. When he spoke, it was almost between clenched teeth. "This seems excessive for dancing."

"It's nothing personal. Everybody does it." She began to move with the slow, sensuous beat of the music. In spite of his efforts at control, Kirk felt the beginnings of arousal. He discreetly moved his hips away.

"I think I get the hang of it. We can stop now."

"The music's just beginning. And it's very beautiful." She smiled up at him. "Dancing is such a simple pleasure. Let's not miss a single minute of it."

At that moment, with Joanna smiling up at him and her fragrant body pressed into his arms, Kirk would have slain dragons for her. Knowing that what he was about to agree to was dangerous, knowing that it would only fan the flames that burned him, he agreed to continue the dance.

"You're right. Dancing is a simple pleasure. One I'd never noticed before." Taking the lead, he swayed across the floor with her.

"You don't need teaching, Kirk. You're a natural."

"Only with you."

She leaned her head against his chest, and the subtle fragrance of her hair drifted around him. From that moment on he knew he would never smell jasmine without wanting her.

"Only with you," he whispered.

Chapter Five

The music played on. Outside the evening sky had darkened and a summer rain began to fall.

Joanna had the strange feeling that she was on a movie set, acting out a role. She had offered to teach Kirk to dance merely as a means of helping him get some enjoyment from life. Her motives were lofty—friendship and genuine concern. The lesson had started with the best of intentions. But something had gone awry. Dancing in his arms made her feel dreamy and happy. This is what she imagined romance felt like—two lovers, pressed close, cherishing the moment and each other.

She glanced at him from under her lashes. There was a determined expression on his face, as if he were enduring some private torture. She was vaguely disappointed. She didn't know what she had expected; perhaps the same sort of contentment she felt. That was foolish, of course. He viewed her as a child, a responsibility.

Sighing, she lifted her head off his chest, resolving to capture every nuance of pleasure from the dance, no matter what Kirk felt.

"This is almost like pretending, isn't it?"

"What's that, Joanna?" The look he gave her was distracted. "I'm afraid I was concentrating so hard on getting the steps right, I wasn't listening."

"Do you remember when you were sixteen and I asked you to be my Prince Charming?"

He smiled. "Yes. It was a rainy weekend. We were both here with Grandfather Deerfield. You had a new book of fairy tales and you conned me into acting out the parts with you."

"You kissed me."

"Only on the cheek, and at your strict instructions."

"It's raining outside now, Kirk."

"I know."

She felt his arms tighten around her, felt every hard place of his body as he pulled her close and rested his chin on her head. Closing her eyes, she pretended that she and Kirk were lovers. She pretended that they would dance long after the music had ended, reluctant to let each other go. Then they would cuddle up in the candlelight and do the things that lovers do—whatever those things were.

It was a beautiful dream.

"Kirk?"

"Hmm?"

"Kiss me again."

He moved back from her, and his steps became stiff and awkward.

"We're too old to pretend, Joanna."

"Then don't pretend. Teach me, Kirk."

"You don't know what you're asking of me."

"You told me that you're older and more experienced. Teach me what love is like."

"I'm not suited for that job, Joanna."

"Then who is? Mother left me in the custody of Grandfather Deerfield so she could flit around the world. She never had time to talk to me about anything more significant than the latest fashions in Paris. And Grandfather Deerfield probably thought I'd find out about love on my own. You're all I have, Kirk."

"You have Sophie."

"Aunt Sophie and Uncle Kenneth are out of town. You know that. Please, Kirk. How can I know whether I'm falling in love with Alfred...." She stopped speaking and gazed up at him. His eyes, usually so clear she could see her reflection, had darkened till they were the gray of storm clouds. A small muscle twitched in the corner of his jaw. She wanted to put her hand on his fine square jaw and smooth the twitch away. A week ago she would have made that simple gesture and thought nothing of it.

She felt confused—elated and scared at the same time. Her tongue flicked out and wet her dry lips. Taking a deep breath, she continued, "... or whether I'm falling in love with someone else?"

"Aw, Joanna." His words were half groan, half sigh. Taking her hand, he led her toward the sofa. He sat for a while, studying her. She was acutely aware of the heat of his hand on hers, of the sensual pulse of music around them.

He turned her hand over and caressed her palm. "Love is very complicated. I'm not sure I can find the right words to describe it."

"Passion, desire, sexual fulfillment." She used all the words she'd read in magazines.

"Love is more than one set of hormones calling to another."

"But the magazines say sex is a big part of love."

"Of course sex is a part of it." He jumped up from the sofa and began to pace.

"You're going to wear a hole in the Oriental rug."

He passed by the stereo and viciously punched the button. The music came to an abrupt halt. "How can I think with that damned music playing? It sounds like a French bordello in here."

"I thought the music was lovely. I thought you were enjoying it."

"Don't look so crestfallen. Is that a tear in your eye?" He crossed swiftly to her and knelt beside the sofa. Taking her face between his hands, he crooned to her, "Please, baby. Don't cry. You look like a flower that's been stepped on. I'm sorry, sweetheart. I didn't mean to be so gruff."

"It's not your fault. It's me. Life is so complicated."

"So is love, Joanna. It's respect and admiration and genuine caring. It's being partners and best friends and lovers. It's laughter and tears and joy so great it wells up and spills over."

"That's beautiful, Kirk."

"So is your smile." He kissed her cheek and stood up. "Are you all right?"

"Yes. You always seem to make everything all right."

It was true, she thought. No matter how angry she got at Kirk for being bossy and domineering, she always turned to him with her problems. And he had never let her down. With her spirits completely restored, she stood up and hugged him.

"Why don't we get a big pizza and some popcorn and rent enough movies to have an all-night binge? Just like old times."

"I'm sorry, Joanna." He set her firmly aside. "I have other plans. Don't wait up for me."

She watched him go. He walked swiftly, like a man with a purpose. Probably a purpose named Marsha. Jealousy slashed through her. Then disappointment. And finally a sense of reality.

"Well, Joanna. What did you expect? That he'd change his whole life-style simply because you came back to town? He's used to women of sophistication and experience. Not wide-eyed innocents who don't know love from hormones."

Saying the words aloud gave her a noble feeling of martyrdom. She wallowed in the feeling for five minutes, then she became bored with herself. She certainly wasn't going to waste the evening moping.

The car keys jingled as she got them out of the hall table. Then, climbing into Kirk's navy Oldsmobile, she went to the Seven-Eleven. She scanned the racks for every magazine that was even remotely connected to love and marriage. With her arms loaded, she headed back home.

Kirk had no clear-cut plans. All he knew was that he had to get out of the house. Dancing with Joanna had made him all too aware of her as a woman. He feared the situation would become explosive if he stayed near her for the rest of the evening.

He dressed quickly, then picked up the phone. He'd call Marsha. Maybe even spend the night with her. They'd had a pleasant affair since his divorce, though it had been nothing to set the world on fire. In fact, the affair had quickly fizzled to an easy friendship. Sex hadn't been a part of their relationship in nearly a year. Still, they were comfortable with each other. Tonight, if things should lead to the bedroom, he'd certainly not object.

He dialed three digits of her number, then slammed the phone receiver down, cursing. What kind of selfish brute was he? Using one woman to forget another? Two wrongs didn't make a right. He was wrong to be feeling anything except protective toward Joanna, and he was equally wrong to be thinking of taking his sexual frustration out on Marsha.

He jerked off his tie and flung it across the bed. If he'd had a punching bag handy, he'd have pulverized it. He felt trapped, helpless. It was a feeling similar to the one he'd had during his marriage to Belinda. And it was a feeling he hated. Not having full control of any situation was anathema to him.

He strode from his room and down the stairs. When he picked up the Lincoln keys, he noticed the ones to the Oldsmobile were missing. Joanna had probably taken them. Who could blame her for leaving? He'd certainly provoked her. It was too late to do anything about that now. He'd let that get out of his control, too. If she did anything drastic, he'd have it on his conscience.

As he got into the Lincoln, his whole body felt tense, even his scalp. His mood matched the murky damp weather that had settled in after the rain. He was fit company for neither man nor beast. The best thing he could do was hole up somewhere, like a sick man in quarantine.

He turned his car toward the all-night drive-in movie.

Kirk's Lincoln was gone when Joanna got back from the Seven-Eleven. She pretended it didn't matter.

The house was empty, and she had no one to talk to about her problems. She felt an intense longing for her mother—for her love, her approval, her presence. She longed for an ordinary mother-daughter relationship. She longed for her mother to be a part of her life, to share the small triumphs and small defeats. But Janet was gone—in Rome, according to her last postcard. Joanna pretended that didn't matter, either.

Taking her magazines, she went to the kitchen and made herself a huge bologna sandwich, one with plenty of mayonnaise and lettuce and pickles. Then she spread her reading material across the kitchen table and settled in for a crash course in romance.

She pored over the pages. Never had she known there were so many ways to please a man. And all of them were set forth as rules. Her dander rose immediately. She hated rules. Some of them made sense, though. For instance, she could understand how looking one's best would please a man, or anybody else, for that matter. But she'd be darned if she knew why mending a man's underwear was so all-fired important. Why didn't he just throw the ratty old things away and buy some new ones? Or mend them himself?

The suggestions for pleasing a man in the bedroom excited her imagination. Some of them even made her blush. She flipped quickly past those pages.

"No sense in trying to master all that stuff, Rags. I have to catch him first."

Her conversation didn't even wake Rags from his dream. He lay in his dog basket, legs twitching in imitation of chasing a rabbit.

Joanna turned back to her research, cocking her head occasionally to catch any sounds indicating Kirk's return. The nighttime creakings of the house were all she heard.

Around midnight Joanna moved her stack of magazines upstairs. She read an article called "For Whom the Bed Tolls" while she was in a tubful of bubbles. Then she dressed for bed and fell asleep over "Six Easy Lessons for Vamping a Man."

* * *

Kirk studiously avoided Joanna the rest of the weekend. He kept himself fully occupied until Monday, working and running errands—even inventing them when necessary. And then he could no longer avoid her. When he came down to breakfast, she was dressed and ready to go to work at Deerfield Manufacturing.

"You're up early, Joanna."

"I wanted to make darned sure I didn't miss you. You've been a phantom all weekend."

"I've been busy. Have you had breakfast?"

"Yes. Rose was already here when I got up. She's made some for you, too."

"Join me and we'll discuss business." As she sat down he noticed that she'd passed over her usual flamboyant outfits, brightly colored sundresses and rows of bangle bracelets, in favor of a simple navy-blue linen dress with a white collar. "You look nice today, Joanna. Very appropriate."

"I'm not sure I like appropriate, but I do want to make a good impression on my first day at work."

"You know the terms of Grandfather Deerfield's will?"

"I vaguely remember them. I'm not sure I understand it in connection with the business, though."

"Deerfield Manufacturing is a closed corporation. I own fifty-one percent; you own forty-nine. I'm the designated manager, in perpetuity, with full voting control of your stock until, in my judgment, you are capable of voting your own."

"That could be never."

"Exactly."

She was thoughtful for a moment. And when she spoke, he was pleasantly surprised at her attitude. "Grandfather Deerfield was a wise man. He knew that you'd protect my interests as zealously as you'd protect your own. I'd be foolish to think I could waltz into Deerfield and start giving orders simply because I'm part owner. I may be young, Kirk, but I'm not dumb. I want to learn, not take charge."

"Then I'll teach you. And I want you to feel free to suggest changes and improvements. You *are* one of the owners. I believe any company benefits from innovation." Kirk relaxed for the first time since she'd shown him the slow dance. Where business was concerned, he was in full command. There was nothing mysterious or frustrating to him about Deerfield Manufacturing. In that familiar and comfortable territory, he could handle anything, even teaching Joanna.

After they'd arrived at the plant, he gave her a complete tour, introducing her to the employees and explaining their product lines. He noted with satisfaction that she listened carefully and asked intelligent questions. And he took pride in the employees' reactions to her. She charmed them, which didn't surprise him in the least.

Back in his suite of offices, he introduced her to his private secretary. "I'm going to put you in the hands of Karen—at least for a few days. She knows everything that goes on, and she can help you get a feel for the business."

To Karen, he said, "As you know, Joanna is the other stockholder. Confidentiality is no problem."

"You leave everything to me, Mr. Maitland. I'll take good care of Miss Deerfield."

"If there are any problems, I'll be in my office."

"Call me Joanna," he heard her say as he closed his door. Everything was going to work out fine, he decided.

Joanna took an immediate liking to Karen. She was tall and slim and efficient-looking. She fairly sparked with energy. With her long legs, long face and trim gray hair, she reminded Joanna of a greyhound who was a veteran of the racetrack.

"I hope you have a magic wand to wave over me. I'm afraid I'm totally ignorant of anything connected with business. Especially machines." She wrinkled her nose at the computer on Karen's enormous polished desk.

"We'll master those in no time flat." Karen took Joanna's arm and led her to a small table. "We're going to start small and work up to the big stuff. Material to be filed is here. I'm going to explain my filing system, then I want you to read this correspondence before you file it. That way you can learn a little of what goes through this office. Later on I'll have a personal computer sent up for you so you can really get your feet wet."

Joanna worked hard. She was determined to learn as quickly as she could. By the end of the day she'd made three discoveries: her background had left her abysmally unprepared for big business; her artistic nature rebelled at so much scheduling and precision; and Kirk was a dynamo, cramming so much work into one day that she rarely saw him except when he passed through the reception area of his office suite.

By the time the day had ended, Joanna was exhausted.

Even Kirk noticed. As they walked to his car, he noticed that her usual jaunty step was missing. "Poor baby. You're tired."

She leaned her head back against the seat. "I've never worked so hard in my life." She sat quietly while he started the car and headed out of the parking lot toward home. "I don't think I can move, let alone eat."

"I'm sorry the day was so long for you, Joanna. Tomorrow we'll go in separate cars so you won't have to wait until my conferences are over."

"Do you work until eight o'clock every day?"

"Not every day."

"But most?"

He grinned. "Yes. I thrive on challenge."

He seemed to thrive on hard work, too, Joanna thought as the car pulled into Meadowlane. He seemed as full of vitality as he'd been that morning. She didn't understand how he could do it. She felt that her legs could barely carry her into the dining room.

Rose had left dinner for them. The sight of the crystal and china, sparkling against the snowy tablecloth, and the delicious aroma of lobster newburg restored her spirits.

Joanna ate her meal with gusto. Watching her, Kirk laughed.

"I thought you were too tired to move."

"Food always revives me."

"I'd forgotten that."

"There are a lot of things you've forgotten. Chess, for instance. We haven't had a good game since I got home. Let's play after dinner."

"Sorry. I have work to do."

Up until now she'd thought his work at home was necessary. But it suddenly occurred to her that he might be using it as a means of escape. She wasn't naive enough to think he needed to escape from her, but she wondered if he felt the need to escape from relationships in general. Maybe he was carrying some scars from his marriage to Belinda. Privately, Joanna had always thought she was a witch. She remembered that Kirk had described himself as being a boring husband. That witch had probably done something to make him think so. Or maybe Marsha, that ice-cool lawyer number, was giving him some trouble. Her concern for him overrode the usual surge of jealousy she felt when she thought of Marsha.

Joanna sighed. Whatever her other feelings for Kirk were—and she'd be darned if she could figure it all out— first and foremost, she was his friend.

"Do you want to talk about something, Kirk? You can tell me anything."

Her reward was the pleased expression on his face. "That's always been true, hasn't it, Joanna?"

"Yes." She reached across the table for his hand.

He lifted her hand to his lips for a brief kiss, then released her. "Thanks for the offer, but not this time. This is something I have to work out by myself."

"Then, do you mind company tonight?" She saw the strained look on his face, and before he could say no, she hurried on. "I have a good book to read. If you don't mind, I think I'll bring it to your study."

"I always enjoy your company, Joanna, but..."

"I'll be quiet as a mouse. I promise."

He stood up. "When you turn on that high-voltage smile, I can never deny you. Bring your book into my study."

It was so late, Joanna decided to bathe and dress for bed before she joined Kirk. Anyway, reading always put her in the mood for sleep. On the other hand, baths usually woke her up.

She poured bath oil into the tub—jasmine, her favorite—and soaked in the bubbles for a while. Then, humming a jazzy tune, she put on her gown. It was black with alternating panels of lace and satin, and it fit like sin on a fallen angel. The matching robe was designed for beauty, not for cover. Joanna loved pretty, feminine clothes, and she adored the feel of satin against her skin. She was smiling when she picked up her book and started for the door.

Suddenly a line from the magazine article about vamping your man came to her: "Always dress as if sex is the ultimate goal.'' Her hand faltered on the doorknob. Although she hadn't consciously set out to vamp Kirk, she was certainly dressed for the part. Deep down, was that what she wanted? She remembered the way she'd felt when they danced. She recalled the pleasure of his kiss. Of course, she'd initiated the dance and goaded him in to the kiss, but that didn't change her feelings. She'd felt gloriously happy and content. She'd felt warm inside, as if a shining flame had been lit next to her heart. And she'd felt a strange, exciting tension, as if her body knew something her mind did not.

Joanna pressed her hands to her temples. If she really knew what falling in love felt like, she'd say that's what was happening to her. Joy welled up inside her. Then, hard on its heels came confusion. All the reasons she shouldn't fall in love with Kirk Maitland came pouring into her mind. They were separated by more than age; they were separated by life-styles. He was so straitlaced and businesslike, her harum-scarum ways would drive him crazy. He needed somebody sophisticated and settled. In addition to all that, she was his cousin—in his eyes and in the eyes of the world. Psychologically, they would have to make a quantum leap to overcome that relationship.

She felt like crying, but what good would that do? Self-pity was a waste of time. Besides, Kirk was downstairs waiting for her. If she didn't show up he'd probably stalk upstairs like some great jungle beast to find out what was going on. There was only one thing to do: try to stop falling in love before it got out of hand.

Joanna pulled off her black lace robe and substituted the old blue terry-cloth one. It was just as well that she could never have Kirk, she rationalized. He was too domineering. She certainly didn't intend to be bossed around the rest of her life.

Picking up her book, she marched resolutely downstairs to Kirk's study. Then she pushed open the door and
went inside—bravely, as if she were accustomed to facing
lions.

When she came through the door, the first thing Kirk
noticed was the scent of jasmine. The heady fragrance
sparked such a burst of desire within him that he was
thankful to be sitting behind his desk. The brief glimpse of
black satin and lace hanging below the edge of her robe
didn't help, either. Fighting for control, he took a deep,
steadying breath.

She glided silently by, never even glancing his way. It was
just as well. He feared his face might have given him away.

With an effort he dragged his mind back to the project
on his desk. From time to time the fragrance of jasmine
wafted to him across the room, compelling him to glance
up. Joanna was sitting in the wing chair, her head bent over
a book. Finally the brief glances weren't enough. He
looked up from his work and frankly studied her. True to
her word, she was being quiet as a mouse. There was a
dignity in her silence that he'd never noticed before. There
was tranquility, too, the kind of peacefulness a man could
enjoy.

For a moment he allowed himself to fantasize. Joanna
by his side at Meadowlane. Permanently. The vision gave
him intense pleasure. He leaned back in his chair and
smiled, watching Joanna and basking in the warmth of her
presence. He loved the way she tipped her head to one side
when she turned the pages, as if she were trying to peek
ahead to find out what was going on before she could read
it. When she did that, she exposed the soft hair at the nape
of her neck. He felt such an urge to press his lips to that
tender neck and soft hair that he almost left his chair.

Fortunately his common sense prevented him. Fool, he raged at himself. She's even younger than Belinda. Wasn't one mistake enough for you?

He sought a hold on reality by speaking to her.

"What are you reading, Joanna?"

The sound of his voice startled her. Her head jerked up, then she smiled.

"Steinbeck. *East of Eden*. It's very good."

"I know."

"You've read it?"

He chuckled. "Does it surprise you that I read?"

"No. Only that you take the time."

"I keep a book tucked into my briefcase to read when I'm flying."

"I like to talk when I'm flying."

"You would."

"There's always somebody with a fascinating story sitting beside me."

Kirk laughed. "Even if somebody told you about the bandage on his sore toe, you'd find some reason to be fascinated. Life fascinates you, Joanna."

"Yes, it does." Shifting in her chair, she put her thumb between pages to hold her place and closed the book. "Am I bothering you, Kirk? I'll leave if I am."

"No. Go ahead with your reading."

He picked up a report that didn't make a damned bit of sense. Probably because his mind was still on Joanna. Did she bother him? she'd asked. If she knew how much she was bothering him and in what way, she'd probably run from the room in sheer panic. Good lord! He raked his hand through his hair. When Joanna had shifted in her chair, the top of her robe had gaped open. The view he'd seen would make angels revolt. Black satin against silky flesh ought to be declared a lethal weapon.

He forced his attention back to his work. By dint of an iron will, he was able to shut Joanna out of his mind. For a long while, there was no sound in the study except the gentle rustle of paper and an occasional sigh from Joanna. When he looked in her direction again, she was slumped in her chair, fast asleep.

"Poor baby. I've worn you out." She didn't even stir. Kirk put his report into his briefcase and walked to Joanna's chair. Smiling, he took the book from her limp hand and placed it on the marbletop table beside her chair. He considered waking her, but finally decided to carry her upstairs to bed. He rationalized that his decision had nothing to do with his desire to feel her in his arms. He told himself it was the least he could do after keeping her so late at the office.

When he picked her up, the heavy terry robe slipped completely away from the satin. She made a stunningly sensual burden.

"Call me a damned voyeur, but I can't help myself." Kirk feasted his eyes on her, reveled in the feel of her. She was all soft womanly curves and enticing hollows. The fluttering pulse at her delicate throat begged for his attention. In spite of his mind screaming "forbidden," he pressed his lips there. The delicious fragrance of jasmine wafted over him. He'd intended the touch to be fleeting, a brief stolen pleasure; but he couldn't get enough of her. With his lips still burning against her throat, he inhaled her scent. His tongue licked at her sweet flesh. Taking a great ragged breath, he lifted his head. "Why in hell couldn't you be ten years older and anybody in the world except a Deerfield?"

"What?" Joanna's voice was sleepy as she squinted up at him. "I must be dreaming." Her right hand curved around the back of his neck. Closing her eyes, she pressed her lips against his. "Hmm, delicious," she murmured.

Kirk knew he shouldn't kiss her back. He knew she didn't know what she was doing. His struggle with his conscience was brief and valiant, but in the end, he lost.

He took her mouth hungrily. The taste of her lips spurred him on. He felt like a starving man, too long denied sustenance. As he devoured her lips, he shifted her so that her breasts were pressed into his chest. Her satin gown enhanced the sensuality.

Desire ripped through him. The hot sweetness of her lips unleashed a primitive beast in him. He wanted her. Now. On the floor. On the sofa. Anywhere. His urge was elemental and as old as time. He simply wanted the delectable woman in his arms.

Her lips came alive under his, responding with a wild passion that was delicious madness. He couldn't have stopped if he had wanted to. He pulled her so close he could feel her nipples through their clothes. They were tight, hard buds that seared his chest. With an agonized groan, he parted her lips, plying that honeyed territory with his tongue, thrusting in a steady rhythm that imitated lovemaking. She opened for him, drawing him deep into her mouth.

There was no sound in the room except their harsh breathing. For once in his life, Kirk lived for the moment. Yesterday was forgotten, and tomorrow was still a dream. Without thinking of the consequences or propriety or control or anything else that ruled his life, he took the pleasure that Joanna offered.

In the hallway the grandfather clock struck twelve. The dramatic marking of time brought a sense of reality back to Kirk. He jerked his head away from Joanna.

"Oh, God, baby. I didn't mean to do that."

She tenderly cupped his face. "Don't look so stricken. I enjoyed it."

"You knew what you were doing?"

"Not at first, I think. I'm not sure. Maybe I did." She smiled up at him. "Anyhow, it didn't take me long to wake up. You sure can kiss."

"Please don't mistake what it was."

"What was it?"

"Temporary insanity."

"Maybe you should strive to make it a permanent condition."

"I'm glad you can make jokes."

"I wasn't joking; I was serious."

Behind that bright smile, he couldn't tell whether she was serious or not. He hoped she was being her usual teasing self. He'd never forgive himself if he hurt Joanna. Gently he set her on her feet.

"Joanna, what happened here tonight won't happen again. I promise you that." She looked so young standing before him, her face flushed and her hair disheveled. He wanted to reach out and smooth that soft hair back from her face. But touching her once more would be a mistake. He wasn't sure he could let her go again.

"Are you sorry it happened?"

The question was a double-edged sword. Either answer would be wrong. Yes would imply he hadn't enjoyed it, and no would seem callous. He reached for her hand.

"Joanna, you're a beautiful woman who deserves a very fine man. And I'm convinced you'll find that man and be extremely happy. That's what I want for you. Happiness."

She smiled. "Well, I'm working as fast as I can to get it."

"Good." He released her hand. "And now that you're fully awake, you can get to bed under your own steam."

"Party pooper. I like being carried around."

"Then you'll have to find someone else to carry you. I'm bushed."

"Poor old honey bear." Standing on tiptoe, she kissed his cheek. "Good night, Kirk."

He was too busy cursing himself to reply. As the door closed behind her, he realized that he was a lucky man. Joanna had handled the awkward situation in an easy manner that had let him completely off the hook. She hadn't held him accountable for his rash behavior, nor had she tried to read romance into it. She'd shown more maturity than he had.

He locked his desk drawer and turned off the lights, thinking all the while that he'd lost control with Joanna tonight. As he left his study, he vowed it would never happen again.

Joanna heard his footsteps as he passed her bedroom. She felt like crying. Downstairs, for one brief moment she'd thought Kirk might actually care for her as a woman. But when he'd looked so stricken, she'd realized her mistake. He'd probably been using her as a substitute for Marsha. Or maybe he was just so tired he hadn't known what he was doing. She hoped she'd saved face for both of them by making light of the kiss. One thing was certain: if she wanted to forget about falling in love with Kirk, she'd darned sure better stop kissing him like that. She'd thought she could exercise more control. Then at the first opportunity she was all over him. And how she had enjoyed it! The thought of letting him go made her feel as if a stone had been laid on her heart.

She'd never known that falling in love could hurt. The magazines didn't tell you that. They didn't tell you what to do if you were attracted to the wrong man. They didn't say how to handle loving a man who didn't love you back.

"Hellfire and damnation." She picked up a pillow and flung it across the room. But neither the defiant words nor the defiant gesture helped.

Chapter Six

Kirk had already gone to work when Joanna got up. There was a note on the kitchen table telling her to take the other car.

When she arrived at work, Karen was waiting with a full list of instructions from Kirk.

"Good morning, Joanna. Mr. Maitland told me to give you these reports to read." She handed Joanna a stack of papers that would have stretched from Tupelo to Natchez. "He's also set up a meeting for you at three with the marketing-and-development department. Grace Crebbs, who heads that department, will explain its work to you. And Mr. Oakland will be taking you to lunch."

Joanna smiled. "How nice. Has Alfred been by this morning?" Yesterday she'd seen him only briefly as she'd passed through the accounting department.

"No. Mr. Maitland arranged the luncheon."

"It's a business lunch, then? Who else will be there?"

Karen quickly consulted her calendar. "There are no business lunches scheduled for today. I can only assume that Mr. Maitland is making sure you're properly taken care of. He considers you top priority."

He was throwing her at Alfred, Joanna thought. She squelched the urge to storm into Kirk's office to do battle. Instead she took a deep breath and smiled at Karen.

"Thank you, Karen. I know you have a lot of work to do without having to take care of me."

"Teaching you is a pleasure, Joanna—and an unexpected one, at that. The thing that makes this job so exciting is that it never stays the same. Mr. Maitland is a brilliant man. He's always coming up with new ideas. You read the file on the Granlan Company yesterday?"

"Yes. Kirk's planning to acquire that company, isn't he?"

"The merger is already in the works. It will expand Deerfield's operations to the Western states."

"We're primarily a Southern company now?"

"Southeastern. We have branches in twelve states." Karen pulled a folder out of the files. "Here. Look through this when you have time."

Joanna glanced from the folder to the stack of reports Kirk had left for her to read. "There's so much to learn."

"Be patient, Joanna. Rome wasn't built in a day."

By lunchtime Joanna was certain that Rome wasn't built in a thousand years. She figured it would take her at least that long to know what was going on in Deerfield Manufacturing. When Alfred stopped by to pick her up, she was more than ready to leave.

"I have a staff meeting at one, so my lunch hour will be strictly that. Is the company cafeteria all right with you, Joanna?"

"Yes. I ate there with Karen yesterday. The food is excellent, although I can't say the same for the decor."

They selected a table in a small alcove.

"I understand this is a command luncheon date."

Alfred laughed. "The boss must have read my mind. I had every intention of calling you for a lunch date."

"But not today?"

"No. Tomorrow, when I don't have to be back at one. How about it?"

"If you don't mind listening to a recital of woes, you're on."

"You have woes, Joanna? Nobody would ever guess by looking at you. You're the picture of sunshine and happiness."

"All I need are a few bluebirds over my shoulder and you could put me in a Walt Disney movie, huh?"

"Something like that. I suppose Deerfield Manufacturing has overwhelmed you."

"In some ways it has. I don't believe my mind is geared for big business, and I certainly don't have the background for it."

"You studied in Spain. Art, if memory serves me."

"It serves you very well. Not only did I acquire a taste for Picasso and Goya and Velázquez, I also acquired a taste for the siesta. I was so tired last night that I fell asleep in my chair."

"It's no wonder, if you tried to keep up with the boss. Kirk Maitland can work circles around all of us."

Joanna gave a dramatic sigh. "All Kirk thinks about is work. That and getting me properly paired with you."

"I don't object. Although it might be more fun to do it my own way."

"What way is that?"

"I believe you put in a request for hearts and flowers and violins. I was thinking in terms of a serenade beneath your window. You could lean out and throw roses at me. Or rocks. Whichever is appropriate."

Joanna laughed. "You've made me forget my woes."

"I'm glad." He reached across the table and took her hand. "Now, would you mind telling me what my reception would be if I appeared beneath your bedroom window."

"It sounds wonderfully romantic, Alfred, and I love music . . ."

"But?"

"I didn't say that."

"I distinctly heard reservations in your voice. It's my nature. I have an eye and an ear for subtle detail."

"Would I invite you up to my bedroom? The answer is—"

"Joanna. Alfred." Both looked up to see Kirk approaching their table. "Enjoying your lunch?"

"Certainly. Joanna makes everything enjoyable."

"Do I get a gold star if I say yes and a demerit if I say no?" Joanna felt a little breathless with Kirk standing over her. She could also feel her heart racing. Two signs of love, according to *Super Romance* magazine.

Kirk laughed. "I'm glad to see you feeling so spunky today."

"Is there any reason why I shouldn't?"

"You *did* fall asleep in your chair."

Kirk gave her a long look that fairly sizzled. Was he remembering what had happened afterward? she wondered. Worse yet, was he seeing in her eyes that she wanted it to happen again? She'd read in *Psychology of Our Times* that the eyes were the windows to the soul. She thought she'd better pull the blinds down over her windows, but she couldn't. Just looking at Kirk gave her intense pleasure. Today she was seeing him in a way she never had. She was seeing him through the eyes of love, memorizing every small detail.

"Dozing in the chair is hardly strenuous. And it's certainly nothing to lose sleep over."

"Then you slept well?"

"Like a rock. And you?" She wasn't about to admit that she'd tossed and turned so much she thought she'd have to cut her way out of the sheets this morning. She could be as cool and sophisticated as Marsha when she put her mind to it.

"I've trained myself to sleep well, no matter what happens. Loss of sleep cuts down on work efficiency. You two have a good time." He wheeled around abruptly and left.

Joanna felt like throwing her water glass after him. Instead she balled her napkin into a wad in her lap. "We've been commanded to have a good time, Alfred."

Alfred made a steeple of his hands as he watched her across the table. He seemed to be in deep thought. "Joanna, what's going on between you two?"

"I've told you. He's issuing commands. It seems he's determined to throw me at you."

"Yes, I'm aware of that. I think there's something more. I saw the way he looked at you."

"How's that?"

"With desire, Joanna."

Suddenly she felt hot and flushed. "How can you tell?"

"You can tell by looking in a man's eyes. Or a woman's. When a long, deep look is exchanged between a man and a woman, it usually indicates sexual attraction. Or at least interest."

"You must think I'm very dumb."

"No. Charming."

Joanna sighed. Propping her elbow on the table, she cupped her chin. "I don't know what's going on. Sometimes I think I'm falling in love with Kirk. Other times I'd like to box his ears for being so bossy. Most of the time I'm totally confused." She reached across the table and took his hand. "I'm sorry you're right in the middle of all this."

"Don't be. Otherwise, I might not have met you."

"You're a good friend, Alfred. You always make me laugh."

Alfred lifted her hand to his lips. "That's a start, Joanna. Although Kirk Maitland is powerful competition, don't count me out of the game yet. I don't give up easily."

"I'm not a prize to be given to the highest bidder."

"Perhaps you won't go to the highest bidder, but you are a prize." He glanced at his watch. "I hate to be the one to spoil a party, but it's almost time for my meeting."

"Thanks for the lunch, Alfred. You've been very comforting."

"Tomorrow I'm going to try for devastating."

On the way back from lunch, Joanna mused that matters of the heart were extremely complicated. Alfred wanted her and she wanted Kirk and Kirk wanted... Who knew what the devil he wanted. What he *needed*, though, was to be taught a lesson. He'd meddled in her affairs today. She had to let him know, once and for all, that she'd handle matters her own way. She smiled as a plan took shape.

Joanna left work early. Getting home before Kirk was crucial to her plan. She made a quick stop by Wal-Mart, then headed for Meadowlane. The first thing she did was find Rose.

"Rose, I need your help."

"I'll do what I can...as long as it's legal and doesn't run counter to Mr. Maitland's orders."

"It's neither illegal nor contrary to Kirk's orders. Before you go home, I'd like you to set the table for an intimate dinner for two. Use the best china, crystal, silver, the works. We're having a guest."

"That's no problem. Anything else?"

"No. That's all." Joanna walked to the broom closet and brought out the broom.

"I've already done the cleaning."

Joanna grinned. "I'm not going to do the cleaning; I'm getting ready for the dinner party." She patted Rose's cheek. "Don't look so concerned. Everything is going to be perfectly legal."

"When you're around I'm never sure." Rose put the finishing touches on her coconut cake. "Is this guest somebody special?"

"I think so."

"Do you need me to stay and serve?"

"No. This guest is self-sufficient. She requires no help at all."

Rose lifted her eyebrows but made no comment. Curiosity was not one of her vices.

Joanna spent the next hour preparing for the intimate dinner. By the time Rose had gone, everything was in place except the guest of honor. Joanna took care of that small detail just as she heard Kirk's car coming up the driveway.

She met him at the door, smiling.

"Did you have a good day at work?"

"Yes. And how was your lunch with Alfred?"

"Perfectly wonderful."

Her good cheer made Kirk suspicious. She'd looked decidedly rebellious when he'd checked on them in the cafe-

NO COST! NO OBLIGATION TO BUY!
NO PURCHASE NECESSARY!

PLAY "LUCKY 7"
AND GET AS MANY AS SIX FREE GIFTS...

HOW TO PLAY:

1. With a coin, carefully scratch off the silver box at the right. This makes you eligible to receive one or more free books, and possibly other gifts, depending on what is revealed beneath the scratch-off area.

2. You'll receive brand-new Silhouette Romance™ novels. When you return this card, we'll send you the books and gifts you qualify for *absolutely free!*

3. Unless you tell us otherwise, every month we'll send you 6 additional novels to read and enjoy. If you decide to keep them, you'll pay only $1.95* per book. And $1.95 per book is all you pay! There is *no* charge for shipping and handling. There are no hidden extras.

4. When you subscribe to Silhouette Books, we'll also send you additional free gifts from time to time, as well as our newsletter.

5. You must be completely satisfied. You may cancel at any time simply by writing "cancel" on your statement or returning a shipment of books to us at our cost.

*Terms and prices subject to change without notice.

teria. He had expected fireworks from Joanna when he got home.

Taking her elbow, he led her into his study. He wanted to ask her about that snatch of conversation he'd overheard, the part about Joanna inviting Alfred up to her bedroom, but he decided to let well enough alone. She was in a good mood, and the lunch date had worked out according to plan—his plan.

"Let me take your briefcase. You must be tired. Why don't you sit over here and put your feet up?" Joanna looked as if she'd been tapped for sainthood as she pampered and petted him.

Kirk *was* tired, he realized. He hadn't slept well lately. Since Joanna had come home, to be exact. And the business was unusually demanding. He didn't know what her game was, but he allowed himself to go along with it. With his feet propped on a stool, he watched Joanna sit down in the wing chair opposite him. She looked soft and demure, a pose if he ever saw one.

"That dress is lovely, Joanna. It makes you look angelic."

"Thank you. I suppose artists have perpetuated the myth that angels wear white."

He smiled. "Is it a fallacy?"

"Definitely."

"How would you paint an angel?"

"Some in white. The truly angelic ones. But the hellions I'd paint in red and purple."

His smile became broader. "There are angels who are hellions?"

"I think so. Life anywhere would be dull and boring if everybody were exactly alike. I think there must be angels who are mischievous and some who are pranksters and even some who are naughty."

Her smile was so wicked he knew she was up to something. But she was so charming he didn't care. As a matter of fact, he felt exhilarated.

"Being a mere earthbound mortal, I wouldn't know about the heavenly citizens. How did you arrive at those conclusions, Joanna?"

"On occasion, I consort with angels."

He studied her face a moment before answering. "On occasion, I do, too." He loved the pink flush that came into her cheeks.

"Then you're going to love our dinner guest."

"Alfred?"

"Alfred is no angel."

"Where you're concerned, he'd better be."

"Don't roar. You're going to excite Celestine."

"Who's Celestine?"

"Our guest. She's not easily aroused, but your shouting is enough to excite a stick of wood."

"Where is this mysterious guest?"

"In the dining room."

"You've left a guest sitting in the dining room by herself? That's not like you, Joanna."

"She's shy."

"Let's join her and put her at ease. She's probably terrified by now." Kirk stood and reached for Joanna's hand.

"There's something I have to tell you first. About Celestine."

"You might start by telling me where you met her."

"At Wal-Mart. She has a terrible crush on you. So I invited her over for dinner. I won't be eating with you."

"You're playing matchmaker?"

"Yes."

"Joanna, I'm perfectly capable of finding my own dinner dates."

"So am I."

She said the words with quiet dignity. Kirk silently applauded her. "You're referring to the lunch with Alfred, of course."

"I am."

"We'll discuss this after dinner. If you'll excuse me, I don't want to keep my guest waiting any longer."

He left his study and walked quickly to the dining room. When he pushed open the door, he saw the crystal and silver gleaming in the dim light of the candelabra. His guest sat at the far end of the table. He couldn't make out her features from the doorway, but the small glimpse he had confirmed his worst fears. Celestine was the ugliest woman he'd ever seen.

"Hello. I'm Kirk Maitland."

She didn't say a word. Kirk resigned himself to an evening of laborious one-sided conversation. Closing the door, he entered the room.

"Joanna tells me she met you at Wal-Mart. I'm happy...." He stopped in midsentence. His eyes had adjusted to the candlelight and he was close enough to get a good look at his dinner guest. Celestine was a broomstick. Literally. Joanna had made a papier-mâché face, put a wig on the straw end of the broom and dressed it up in a pink shirt, stuffed to look like a body. Kirk walked closer and examined Celestine. She was even wearing slacks and shoes. Her well-endowed figure was stuffed with cotton batting.

Stifling his laughter, Kirk sat down at the table. "As I was saying before I saw your stunning face, I'm happy you could come. Women of your sort always attract me. So compliant and willing. So obedient." He helped himself to the veal. "You don't talk much, do you? I like that in a woman. The quiet kind. Gives a man time to think. Have some carrots. Nobody prepares them quite like Rose.''

He carried on the one-way conversation in a very loud voice, for he was absolutely certain Joanna was lurking close by to find out his reaction. She'd probably expected him to come barging from the dining room like a wounded bull. Then she probably expected they'd come back into the dining room and have a long discussion over a hot meal. He chuckled. The whole thing was amusing to him. As a matter of fact, he hadn't had this much fun in years.

He lingered over the meal, sipping the wine slowly while loudly extolling its merits to Celestine.

Outside in the hallway, Joanna was getting hungry. She'd followed discreetly behind Kirk to get his reaction. And it had been totally unexpected. She'd expected a roar of anger. Or a roar of laughter. But he'd done neither. As a matter of fact, he was sitting in there having dinner with that broomstick while she sat out in the hall and starved. Nobody played these games by the rules.

"I do enjoy a woman who can hold her wine," she heard Kirk say. "Women do the darndest things when they drink too much. The other night Joanna..." Kirk's voice faded so that she couldn't hear a thing he said. She pressed her ear to the door, then she suddenly felt foolish. Of course, he *knew* she was out there. He was leading her on.

Two could play that game, she decided. She tiptoed down the hallway and into the kitchen. With visions of veal cutlets and baby carrots dancing in her head, she made a pimento-and-cheese sandwich and poured a glass of milk. She'd sit in the kitchen and wait him out. He'd soon tire of the game. She'd give him ten more minutes, fifteen at the most, then he'd be out of there, clutching Celestine by the throat and calling for an explanation.

Joanna was wrong. She sat in the kitchen an hour, trying to stretch her meager sandwich to fill the time. There was not a sound from the rest of the house. Finally she could no longer stand the suspense. She marched to the dining room to confront Kirk.

He was gone. And so was Celestine.

"What in the world is that man up to?" Joanna stood in the candlelit room for a moment, trying to decide her next move. Kirk was probably holed up in his study, working like mad, the incident of Celestine already forgotten. That explained his absence, but what had he done with poor Celestine?

Joanna walked to his study and found it empty. Curiosity consumed her. She stepped back into the hallway.

"Kirk?"

"In here, Joanna," he called from the parlor.

She pushed open the door, and there he was, sitting on the sofa, sipping a glass of wine and reading the *Wall Street Journal*. Celestine was draped artfully by his side.

"What took you so long?"

"I didn't want to interrupt a blossoming romance."

"Please feel free. These quiet types get boring after a while. She's not even interested in the *Wall Street Journal*."

Joanna picked up her broomstick woman. "Poor Celestine. You're hurt her feelings."

"I'm sure she will recover. I'm not so sure about myself. I almost had a heart attack when I saw her. Seldom have I had dinner with an uglier woman."

Smiling demurely, Joanna propped Celestine on a chair and sat down beside Kirk. "I aim to please."

Kirk chuckled. "I do believe I'm looking at one of those mischievous angels we discussed before dinner."

"Perhaps even one of the hellions."

"It could be." Cupping her chin with one hand, he gazed thoughtfully at her. "I understand why you brought Celestine to dinner, Joanna."

"You do?"

"Yes. It was a very clever revenge. One I richly deserved, I might add."

"You're not angry?"

"On the contrary. I enjoyed the evening immensely. I don't know when I've had so much to laugh about."

Joanna turned and spoke to the broomstick dummy. "Celestine, did you hear that? You're a hit."

"So are you, Joanna." Kirk kept his hold on her face. "I owe you an apology." He loved the way her dark eyes lit in the center when she smiled. "I had no right to arrange that lunch date for you. You're a beautiful young woman who is perfectly capable of getting Alfred or anyone else to take you out. I'm sorry."

"Apology accepted. But I do understand your motives. You were only doing what you do best; you were managing things."

"I make no excuses for myself. And neither should you. You deserve the best."

"So do you, Kirk." The silence was so thick with unspoken words, Kirk could almost taste it. He held her fragile face in his hands while he gazed deep into her eyes. Never had the need to kiss her been so great. He leaned toward her, drawn irresistibly to her lips. When he was only inches away, he stopped.

"You have cheese on your face." His voice was husky, his passion barely controlled.

"Where?"

"There." He moved his hand to the corner of her mouth. Gently he wiped away the cheese. "You take looking good enough to eat seriously, don't you?"

"Yes. Mischievous angels are like that."

"What would a mischievous angel say if a certain old fogy invited her to go roller-skating?"

"Roller-skating? You?"

He laughed. "If the old fogy fits, wear it. Yes, me. Does that surprise you so much? I'm the one who taught you to skate."

"Are you sure? I noticed your briefcase was bulging with papers. I don't want to interfere with your life-style."

"Joanna, I'm beginning to wonder if there isn't more to life than work. I'm asking you to teach me."

She blushed, remembering what she'd asked him to teach her.

"I'll be glad to teach you. But you'll need to change. Nobody except bankers and governors roller-skates in three-piece suits."

"Great. I'll meet you back here in fifteen minutes." He left the parlor, whistling.

Joanna watched him go. She'd pulled many pranks in her lifetime, but she'd never been rewarded for one. She decided that attitude had made the difference. She'd set up her stunt not out of defiance, but out of desire to make her point clear. Instead of being judgmental and accusing, she'd merely been firm.

She smiled in triumph and hurried upstairs to change into shorts.

The roller rink was almost empty.

Kirk knelt in front of Joanna and laced up her skates.

"I remember when you laced on my first pair of skates."

"So do I." He lingered over the chore, holding her leg firmly across his knee. His hand on her bare leg sent shivers up her spine.

"This is just like old times. Right, Kirk?"

"I don't think so. Lately I've come to believe that one can never go back."

"Are you speaking hypothetically?"

"No. From personal experience."

He made no move to release her leg. The heat of his touch spread upward. She felt a pleasant warmth invade her body. Her tongue flicked out and wet her dry lips.

"If you can't go back, then where do you go?"

"Forward, Joanna, to that unknown and scary future."

Reaching out, she touched his face. "I suppose the future wouldn't be so scary with the right person at your side."

"How very wise you are." He stood up abruptly, lifted her to her feet, then turned her in the direction of the rink. "Why don't you warm up out here while I lace my skates?"

Joanna thought if things got any warmer, she'd burst into flames. She did as she said, mainly to keep from throwing her arms around him and making a fool of herself in a public place.

For a while she immersed herself in skating, concentrating on the thud of the rollers against the wooden floor and the feeling of freedom as she raced around the rink. Skating was almost like flying. Her mind went wheeling free, casting off mundane worries and roaming up high in the place of dreams. As her rollers hummed over the floor, she decided that skating was an adult hobby that could very well replace fifty-dollar-an-hour therapy.

Kirk sat on the sidelines, mesmerized by her. Her zest for life took his breath away. The joyful exuberance fairly flowed from her. "No man in his right mind would retreat from that."

"Did you say something, mister?"

He looked up to see a freckle-faced boy about six years old standing beside him.

"Just talking to myself."

"Old folks are crazy." The little boy wobbled off on his skates.

"Out of the mouths of babes."

Joanna spun to a stop near the railing. "Aren't you coming out, Kirk?"

"Yes. I'm just collecting my courage."

She laughed. "You're not scared, are you?"

"No. Just embarrassed. It's been a hundred years since I was on a pair of these things. I'm going to look funny at work tomorrow with a broken leg."

"I'll hold your hand."

He executed a shaky entrance onto the rink, and Joanna reached for his hand. "Role reversal. I like it." He smiled down at her.

"I do, too."

Holding hands, they skated around the rink, staying close to the railing so that Kirk could catch himself if he needed to. By the time they'd made three revolutions, he was steady on his feet. But still he held her hand.

She glanced up at him. "You caught on quickly."

"My skills are rusty, but they're coming back." The music they'd skated to suddenly changed from disco to dreamy. "The 'Skater's Waltz.' Remember that, Joanna?"

"I do. It was my sixteenth birthday. You had a skating party for me, and that was our first dance."

"And my last—until you came back into my life."

Without another word Kirk turned her in his arms and began to waltz across the floor. Some of their steps were wobbly, but they kept the rhythm.

Joanna felt as if she'd entered a dream. She wanted to close her eyes, but she didn't dare for fear she'd miss a single instant of seeing Kirk's face. The stress she'd seen so often was gone. He was relaxed and smiling. His eyes were sparkling, and he seemed to be enjoying himself immensely. The moment took on a bright clarity, and she knew, as surely as if angels had whispered in her ear, that she was in love with Kirk Maitland. It wasn't a feeling that could be deciphered and put in a magazine as a set of rules. It was a deep caring that defied description. His well-being was her well-being, his joy, her joy. No matter what came of it, she'd always cherish the memory of this moment.

She smiled.

"Happy, Joanna?"

"Very."

"I'm glad." He pulled her close, holding her so tightly against his chest that they could barely maneuver their skates. "I'm so glad, baby."

They were still dancing when the lights dimmed.

"Time to go, Joanna."

"Must we?"

"They're closing the place."

"It might be fun to be locked inside."

"You'd get hungry."

"I already am. Let's stop on the way home for food."

"Hamburger? Pizza?"

"No. The biggest banana split in Tupelo, with ice cream piled as high as the steeple on the Baptist Church."

He laughed as he pulled off her skates. "I had a good meal."

"Can I help it if Celestine overstayed her welcome and I had to scrounge around in the kitchen?"

"Serves you right."

They kept up the light banter during the short drive to Finney's and while they ate their banana split.

When they got back home, Kirk let them in. A small lamp was burning on the hall table. The glow spilled over Joanna, backlighting her so that her hair shone like a halo. Kirk's hand was drawn to the brightness. Then his lips were.

With his mouth against her hair, he spoke. "Thank you for a memorable evening, Joanna."

"It was my pleasure."

He stepped back. "I'll see you in the morning."

He left her and walked quickly into his study. Joanna was wonderfully exhausted. She went upstairs for a long, luxurious soak in the bubbles.

Inside his study Kirk snapped open his briefcase and pulled out the file on the new line of sofas he was considering. His mind felt sharp and clear. After an hour he realized that he'd finished the work he'd expected would take all evening.

It was only midnight when he climbed the stairs, an early evening for him. Inside his bedroom he stripped off his shirt and threw it across a chair. His hand was on his belt buckle when he realized there was something he had to do. Tonight, if possible. Otherwise there'd be no rest for him. Glancing across the hall, he saw the light coming from under Joanna's bedroom door. He walked over and knocked.

"Joanna. Are you still awake?"

"Yes. Come in."

He pushed open her door. She was standing in front of her mirror, brushing her hair. She was dressed in white again, a creamy satin gown and robe that clung to her like a jealous lover. The stab of passion he felt was so sharp

and so sudden, he almost cried out. He took a deep breath
to gain control.

"You look like an angel."

She smiled. "Thank you. Is that what you came across
the hall to tell me?"

"No. There's something I have to know, Joanna."

She said nothing, but stood very still, waiting for him to
continue.

"*Would* you invite Alfred up to your bedroom?"

"You were eavesdropping?"

"Not intentionally. I came by to check on you, and I
overheard. Would you?"

"Is that a hypothetical question?"

"No. Personal."

"In that case, it deserves an answer. No, Kirk. I would
not invite Alfred up to my bedroom."

Her answer made him feel ten years younger. "Thank
you for your honesty."

"You're more than welcome."

"Good night, Joanna."

"Night, Kirk."

The angelic vision of Joanna in her ivory satin gown
stayed with him until he slept—the deep, dreamless sleep
of a man at peace.

Chapter Seven

The next morning, when Joanna and Kirk left for work in separate cars, both wore secretive smiles on their faces. Joanna was thinking of an article she'd read in one of Kirk's business magazines, and he was thinking of the surprises he planned for her.

As soon as she got to work she found the magazine and read it again, just to be sure she'd remembered correctly. It confirmed her thinking, so she boldly advanced her plan. Since she didn't have her own office, Karen couldn't help but catch on to what she was doing.

After lunch she ventured to comment, "What you're doing is mighty brave, Joanna. None of the department heads has even initiated a change without Mr. Maitland's specific okay."

"I'm not a department head, Karen. I'm an owner. Besides, Kirk told me to be innovative. That's what I'm doing. I think he's going to be impressed. Don't you?"

"Shocked might be a better word."

"I'll cross that bridge when I come to it. Right now I have to go down and do some poll taking." She left the office with a jaunty wave.

Kirk came out of his office shortly after she'd gone.

"Where's Joanna?" he asked.

"Downstairs."

"When she comes back will you please tell her I've gone home already." His step was light as he, too, left the office.

"Will wonders never cease?" Karen said, then she turned back to her typing.

Joanna was pleased with herself. In one afternoon she'd managed to locate enough equipment to give her plan a trial run. If it worked, then she'd move into the final stages. At last she was making a real contribution to the business. She was doing something Kirk would admire. When she parked Kirk's Oldsmobile in the garage, she was smiling.

He met her at the door wearing a white T-shirt and Bermuda shorts in a shocking shade of yellow. The shirt was damp with sweat, and the shorts were faded at the seams.

"Hello, Joanna."

She looked him up and down. "Big Bird, I presume?"

Kirk laughed. "They're awful, aren't they? I discovered that my wardrobe is terribly lacking in sports clothes. These are holdovers from my college days. A Christmas present from my best friend's aunt Eleanor, if I remember correctly."

"They make a nice change from your business suits. And you left work early. I approve. You need the rest."

"I didn't come home to rest. Come with me. I have a surprise for you." He took her hand and led her through the hall, into the kitchen and down the basement stairs. She smelled the fresh paint before she saw it.

"You're painting the rec room?" she asked.

"Yes. It hasn't been used since you left for college. I thought I'd brighten it up, get it ready for use again."

Half the basement walls were a faded blue and the other half sported a new coat of bright peach paint.

"I love it, Kirk." She kicked off her shoes. "Do you have an extra brush?"

"You're not going to paint in that skirt?"

"I could pull it off." She grinned at him. "But on second thought, I'll go upstairs and change."

She changed into a pair of shorts and a halter top that left very little to the imagination. With that distraction, Kirk knew that he'd get very little painting done.

"I love do-it-yourself projects." Joanna bent over the paint bucket and dipped her brush in. "This is so much more fun than calling in a decorator, don't you think so?" When she straightened up, she was smiling and dripping paint on the floor.

She was so goodnatured and cheerful about the project, Kirk didn't have the heart to tell her. She could drip paint all over the room for all he cared. Just as long as she was happy. He could always hire a decorator to come in and straighten up the mess.

"Absolutely," he agreed.

She swiped a spot on the wall and bent over the bucket once more. "Kirk, you know what I was thinking?"

He watched in fascination as she made another swipe, getting nearly as much paint on herself as she did the wall.

"No. What?"

"I was thinking what fun it would be to do a painting on this wall. Art. Something bright and lively. Clowns and carousels and hot-air balloons. Similar to the works from Picasso's Rose Period.''

"That sounds delightful, Joanna. Paint whatever you want on the walls."

"Won't the children love it!" She made another pass at the bucket, dripping a stream of paint down her bare leg.

"What children?"

"Our children."

"Ours?"

"This home belongs to both of us. I'm going to have children someday. Aren't you?"

"I used to think so. I haven't given it any thought in years."

"Well, I have. I'm going to have lots of children. And they're all going to love these basement walls."

He suddenly felt old. Of course she'd have lots of children, he thought. She was young, vital. Life was just beginning for her. He'd had his chance and blown it. Suddenly, what he was doing seemed foolish to him, a futile effort at trying to be young.

"Joanna, it's getting late. I think I'll knock off and go upstairs for dinner." He put his paintbrush in the stainless-steel basement sink and turned on the water.

"Wait a minute, Kirk. You have paint on your cheek." She walked over to him and reached for his face.

He leaned out of her way, laughing. "Whoa."

"Hold still."

"If you get your hands on me, I'll have paint on more places than my cheek. You should see yourself, Joanna. You look like you've been tie-dyed."

She looked down at herself. Speckles of peach paint dotted her legs, arms and hands, and even her midriff.

"Why didn't you tell me?"

"And spoil all your fun?" Kirk tossed her a clean washcloth. "Don't worry. It's water-base paint. It'll come out."

While Kirk cleaned the brushes Joanna swiped and smeared at her paint splotches.

"It's hopeless, Kirk. I think I'm going to be speckled for the rest of my life."

Kirk took the washcloth, rinsed it and began to work on her left arm. "You always were impatient." He worked at the smudges, stopping frequently to rinse out the washcloth. "See. It's coming right off. All you have to do is keep cleaning the cloth."

He offered her the cloth but she shook her head. "You do it, please. I'll just make a mess."

Cleaning her arms and hands wasn't so bad, but when Kirk bent to clean her midriff he knew he was walking on thin ice. Joanna's midriff was taut and tanned and somehow vulnerable. It took all his willpower to concentrate on the paint spots instead of on the radiant skin. By the time he got to her legs, his T-shirt was soaked with sweat.

She was so still under his hands, so trusting. He felt like a cad for what he was thinking.

At last the chore was finished. Kirk's hands were trembling when he hung the washcloth over the rim of the sink.

"Joanna, I won't be eating dinner with you tonight."

"But you said . . ."

"I know. But I need to go down to the office and get some of my files on Granlan. As a matter of fact, I think I'll work down there a while tonight. Make up for the time I took off this afternoon."

She didn't seem him again until he got to Deerfield the next day. She'd arrived early in order to set her plan in motion. As soon as he came to the office, she greeted him.

"I'm glad you're here."

He quirked his eyebrows. "Early to work, Joanna? Deerfield must be growing on you."

"I came early to get my surprise ready."

He laughed. "I hope it doesn't involve peach-colored paint."

"No. That was yours. This one is mine." She glanced at the clock on the wall. "I hope you can stand waiting ten more minutes. The surprise won't work unless the employees are here."

He laughed. "You're the impatient one in this family. I can wait. Call me when you're ready." He went into his office.

At precisely nine o'clock, Joanna made her rounds of the plant, setting her surprise into motion; then she went upstairs to get Kirk.

Taking his hand, she led him first to the cutting room. "You're going to love this," she said.

He heard the surprise before he saw it. Rock-and-roll music was pouring forth from the cutting room.

"Joanna, what in the world it going on?"

"I read in one of your magazines that there's a correlation between music and productivity. So I decided to give it a try." She flung the door open with a flourish. "What do you think?"

His usually sedate cutting department was transformed. The bolts of cloth were there; the employees were there; the machines were there. Business was going on, but not as usual. Most of the men and women were smiling, and some of them were shimmying and shaking to the music as they performed their jobs.

His initial reaction was to cut off that horrible racket, but seeing Joanna's smiling face, he controlled the urge. "Why, I think it's . . . innovative."

"I took a poll, Kirk. I found out what kind of music the majority of employees in each department like."

"You've done this in every department?"

"Yes. Wait till you see accounting." They left the cutting room and started down the hall. "Everybody in there is just like Alfred. Conservative. They're playing Brahms and Beethoven. But in marketing and development they prefer jazz. Then there's the assembly line. Guess what they like."

"I'm afraid to ask."

"Country and western. 'Help Me Make It Through The Night' and all those wonderful old crying songs."

His smile was rueful. "I can understand the need for a crying song."

The sparkle left her face. "You don't like what I've done?"

Kirk felt like a heel. He stopped beside the water fountain and took her by the shoulders. "Did you do this for me, Joanna?"

"Yes." Her voice was so soft he had to lean down to catch it. "I *did* think the changes might be good for the company, but I did this mostly for you. I wanted you to see..." She hesitated, biting her bottom lip.

"See what?"

"That we're not so different. That I can be *suitable*."

"Ahh, Joanna." He pulled her into his arms, swiftly, without thought. With his face against her hair and his hands gently massaging her back, he reasoned, "Don't change for any man, and certainly not for me."

She tipped her head back so she could look into his face. "Kirk, I—"

"Mr. Maitland! Your secretary told me to wait in your office, but I took a chance on finding you, and there you are." Gracelyn Phillips bore down on them as she talked.

Kirk stepped back from Joanna, but kept his arm protectively across her shoulders. "And is this little Joanna, all grown-up, with you?" The hand Gracelyn offered Kirk was covered with enough jewels to decorate a queen's crown. "My, my. Your little *cousin*, isn't she?" She dramatically emphasized the word cousin by lifting her plucked eyebrows halfway into her lacquered bangs.

"Hello, Gracelyn." Kirk gave her limp hand a brief shake, then turned smoothly to Joanna. "You remember Gracelyn Phillips, don't you? She's the head of every charity fund-raiser in Tupelo." Smiling at Gracelyn, he said, "What can my stepcousin and I do for you today?" His sharp emphasis on stepcousin would have cut through steel.

"I'm working for a good cause, of course, and I do know you'll want to be generous. You always are. And your Granddaddy before you."

"We'll talk in my office. Joanna, do you have time?"

"Yes."

The three of them went into Kirk's office and settled on a generous donation for Gracelyn's latest project. After Gracelyn had gone, Kirk turned his attention to Joanna.

"We never finished our conversation, Joanna."

"No."

The interlude with Gracelyn had allowed him to get the situation back into proper perspective. One disastrous marriage to a much younger woman had been enough. He'd never stifle Joanna the way he had Belinda. With the desk between him and Joanna, he felt more in control. "I'm proud of you for undertaking this project on your own. We'll reserve judgment on it until it's had a trial run."

"All very formal and businesslike."

"Yes."

"And cold."

"Cold, Joanna?"

She rose from her chair and began to pace. "Yes, cold. We used to be such good friends, and now...." She paused and spread her hands wide.

"Nothing ever stays the same."

She walked to his window and looked out over the city. In the four years since she'd been gone, it had grown. As far as she could see, not one lot was vacant. Small businesses had sprung up like mushrooms. Neon signs pointed the way to everything from take-out chicken to brand new Cadillacs. On the hill, the hospital buildings had multiplied like a favorite rabbit. She pressed her face to the glass.

"Everything has changed."

"Change isn't bad, Joanna."

"No, but sometimes it's very hard."

Seeing her turmoil, his heart ached for her. He longed to reach out, to comfort, but he feared what would happen if he did. In spite of his efforts to keep it the same, their relationship *had* changed. Innocent gestures kept getting out of control. Decisive action didn't seem to solve anything. Kirk felt as if he were in a time warp. He was reminded of the days of his marriage, of the frustration of not being able to control the situation.

He sat in his chair, watching Joanna, willing himself to let her go. "Change is damned hard, baby."

She whirled around. "Why do you keep calling me that?"

"I've always called you baby."

"Yes. But not in the way you do now. There's an intimacy in the way you say it."

"You're imagining something that isn't there."

"Am I?"

"Yes." He hated lies. He'd always thought himself above them. But lately everything about his relationship with Joanna was a lie—pretending he didn't want her when it took every ounce of his restraint to keep his hands off her; pretending to endorse her courtship with Alfred when he wanted to punch the man's face every time he came near her; pretending that life at Meadowlane was normal when it was a daily exercise in denial and frustration.

He picked up a file folder that was on top of his desk and flipped it open. "If there's nothing else on your mind, I have work to do."

He watched her straighten her shoulders, lift her chin. "So do I." Her dignified exit would have done Grace Kelly justice. He was seeing a maturity that hadn't been there when she'd returned to Meadowlane. Joanna was definitely a woman, and that was the hardest change of all.

Kirk struck his desk with his fist. He'd be damned if he knew what to do.

After Joanna left Kirk's office, she went straight to the employees' lounge. She didn't want to face Karen; she didn't want to face anybody. Although she didn't care for coffee, she poured herself a big cup. She figured a stiff shot of caffeine might perk her up. It might even stimulate her brain cells so she'd know what to do.

She took a sip, then propped her elbows on her knees and her chin on her fist and stared at the wall.

"The Thinker, I presume?"

She smiled at Alfred standing in the doorway. He came over and sat down beside her. "Is this a private party, or can anyone join?"

"You're always welcome, Alfred."

Putting his finger under her chin, he tipped her face up. "Is the world coming to an end? Where's that big smile?"

She chuckled. "I hardly think the world's going to end because Kirk and I fought."

"I'm a good listener, Joanna."

"I know you are." She reached for his hand. "And a good friend. But nothing's more boring than a recital of woe."

Alfred sat back and studied her. "On a scale of woe, I'd give you about a two, closer to mildly disturbed than wildly woeful."

She laughed. "Alfred, someday you're going to make some woman a wonderful husband."

He put his hand over his heart. "*Some* woman, Joanna? How you wound me. Over lunch today I'll prove that you're the woman."

She became serious. "I should cancel our lunch date. It's not fair to you."

"Not fair to whom?"

"To you."

"Joanna, life is rarely fair, but it sure as hell is exciting. I'll take my chances just like everybody else." He stood up. "I'll pick you up at twelve. Agreed?"

"Agreed."

Kirk saw Alfred and Joanna leave together for lunch, and immediately lost his appetite. He worked straight through the rest of the day until it was so late his vision began to get bleary. When he got home that night, Joanna was already in bed. He thanked God for small favors. He was spared seeing her and not being able to touch her.

In spite of a short night's rest, Kirk woke early Saturday morning, restless and filled with a sense of urgency. As he dressed he cocked his head, listening for sounds of Joanna. Was that the sound of her bare feet on the floor? Did he hear running water? Was she drawing her bath? With his head half in his T-shirt, he stood listening. The house was silent except for the patter of Rags's feet as he went down the hall, probably to his favorite window seat in the sunshine.

The silence meant Joanna was still sleeping. He could picture her in bed, bright hair tousled across the pillow, long eyelashes curving on her soft cheeks. He had to grit his teeth to keep from going across the hall to her. He wanted to touch her face, smooth back her hair. He wanted to be the first thing she saw when she woke up. He wanted to be the reason for her smile.

"Damned fool." He jerked his shirt the rest of the way over his head and went downstairs for a hasty breakfast. Then he disappeared into the basement.

Joanna woke at midmorning, donned her terry-cloth robe and pattered through the house looking for Kirk. She found him in the basement, painting.

"Need some help down here?" she called as she descended the stairs.

"No." He carefully put his brush down and stared at her. That long leg showing through the open front of robe didn't improve his temperament a bit. "Don't come any closer, Joanna."

"Why not?"

Because I'm liable to rip that robe off you and take you right here on the basement floor, he thought. "Because you'll get paint everywhere," he said.

"You needn't be so fierce. Just because I made a small mess the other night—"

"That's just one of the many ways we're different, Joanna." He picked up his brush and returned to his work. His back was stiff and his expression grim.

Joanna started to push the subject, but, seeing his turmoil, she changed her mind and went quietly up the stairs. In the kitchen she sliced strawberries into her cereal and sat down at the kitchen table. The sunshine poured through the windows, but it did nothing to cheer her up. What were they to do? she wondered. Her love for Kirk was a shining joy that she wanted to share. But he kept putting walls between them. There had to be a way to break through.

As she put her bowl into the dishwasher she determined that she would find a way. She'd never let anything defeat her, and she wasn't about to start now.

She put on her swimsuit and went outside in the sunshine to think. Stretched in the lounge chair beside the pool, she let her mind roam free. She'd read that love conquers all. Of course, love had never been up against anybody as strong willed as Kirk. Once he made a decision, nothing could sway him. And he'd certainly made it plain that one mistake with a young woman was enough for him. She'd just have to make him change his mind.

"The sun becomes you, Joanna." She jerked her head around to see Kirk standing near the edge of the pool apron. She'd been so busy thinking, she hadn't heard him approach. With the sun highlighting the silver at his temples, he looked good enough to eat.

"The sun becomes you, too." She swung her arm toward a nearby chair. "Won't you join me?"

As he sat down his gaze swept over her. She was wearing a string bikini she'd bought on the Costa Brava. The look he gave her was so intimate she felt herself blush all the way to the roots of her hair.

"Joanna, I came to apologize for what happened in the basement this morning—and yesterday at the office."

"There's no need."

"Yes. Hear me out, please. My behavior toward you has been less than charitable lately, and I'm sorry."

"No. You're wonderful. You've just been overworked. You work too hard."

"You've made me realize that, too. But please don't make excuses for me. I've let personal problems affect my behavior toward you." He lifted her hand briefly to his lips, then quickly let it drop. "You're precious to me, Joanna. I don't ever want to lose you—" Abruptly he stopped speaking. His gaze sizzled across her, lingering over her legs, her breasts, her face. She felt as if she were being caressed. A warm glow filled her, and if her heart had been a bird, it would have soared.

"You won't," she said softly.

"I don't ever want to lose your *friendship*," he amended quickly. "I should have told you yesterday that I'm proud of you for trying to help Deerfield. Your music project was innovative and bold . . . and it just might work."

"Do you think so?"

"Anything is possible."

If anyone except Kirk had said that, she might have thought it trite. But coming from him, the optimistic philosophy became a powerful statement. *Anything is possible.* She could do it, she vowed. She could make it all work. And she'd do it right. One step at a time. First she'd win his respect. Then she'd win his love.

"Kirk?"

"What have I done to deserve that wonderful smile? You look as if the sun's just risen in your face."

"Are you sincere about wanting my suggestions?"

"Yes."

"I've been listening to the women employees talk. Did you know that many of them have a very hard time taking care of their children and working?"

"Yes. It's a common problem."

"Have you ever thought of providing day care at Deerfield?"

"I haven't, but it does sound like an idea worth considering."

"It might even result in increased productivity. If the women don't have to worry about child care, I think they'll work with more enthusiasm and efficiency."

"We'll start working out the details Monday morning in my office. I'm proud of you, Joanna. You've come a long way from the girl who called balance sheets dull and boring."

"I'm not a girl. I'm a woman."

"A fact that never fails to escape my attention."

She thought the look in his eyes was pure sex. It was strange to her how even the simplest looks and words took on added meaning when a person was in love. She ached to have him touch her, kiss her. She almost reached out to him, but she knew what his reaction would be. One step at a time, she reminded herself.

Sighing, she reached for her suntan oil and began rubbing it on her arms.

"Is something bothering you, Joanna?"

"Why?"

"I can always tell. Your face gives you away."

"Then I'll have to learn not to be so transparent." She poured a dollop of oil on her right palm and slowly massaged her chest.

Kirk envied the oil. To be rubbed so intimately over her breasts would be ecstasy. He longed to bend over her and follow the path of the oil with his lips. As he watched her anoint her body, he was filled with regret.

"Joanna?"

Her hands stilled, and a small dollop of oil tunneled between her breasts. Not touching that glistening skin was agony, Kirk thought. Joanna was still, waiting for him to say what was on his mind, but he restrained himself. With Joanna, nothing had ever been held back. But lately he'd been holding his feelings on a tight leash, careful of everything he said and did around her.

What he wanted to say was, how do you perceive me? Do you think of me as old? It was suddenly very important to him that Joanna not view him as too old. Too old in general? Too old for her? He didn't know.

He pulled his gaze away from that erotic oil on her sun-tanned skin. "We've always been honest with each other, Joanna. Are you sure there's nothing bothering you?"

"It's nothing I can discuss with you, Kirk."

"You've always come to me with your problems. I don't want anything to change that."

"I've discovered that some problems have to be worked out alone. And some of them can't be worked out at all."

"All problems have a solution."

"Do you believe that?"

"Until lately I did."

A lone mosquito buzzed around their heads as they stared at each other. Kirk could sense a struggle in Joanna. He willed her to confide in him, to confess her problems. Maybe in helping her he could help himself.

Suddenly she handed him the bottle of oil and rolled onto her stomach. "Why waste a perfectly gorgeous day talking about problems? Will you do my back?"

Rubbing oil on her back was a chore he had performed many times before. Automatically he took the bottle. He

touched her sun-warmed skin, and something inside him
splintered. For an instant his hands trembled on her back,
then he began a slow, intimate massage. He would take the
moment as a gift and worry about the consequences later.
As his fingers kneaded her soft flesh, he memorized every
sensuous inch of her, the lovely slope of her shoulders, the
fine curves of her back, the tiny nipped-in waist.

"Mmm. Nobody does that quite like you, Kirk. Will
you do my legs?"

Oiling her back had been ecstasy; oiling her legs was
sweet torture. It was a good thing his hands knew what to
do, he decided, for his mind was somewhere else. He
imagined those exquisite legs on a satin sheet, parted for
him. He could almost feel the wet heat of her soft yielding
flesh.

"Damn." The word exploded from him as he jumped
up.

Joanna turned over. "Kirk? Where are you going?"

"To the basement to work on that rec room. I feel the
need to pound something with a hammer."

She stood up. "I'll help you."

"No!" He swung around, scowling. Seeing her crestfallen look, his face softened. "No, thank you, Joanna. I
need to be alone for a while."

After she'd sunbathed, Joanna dressed and went shopping. Spending money gave her something to do besides
mull over unrequited love. Mulling wasn't her style, anyway, and it certainly wouldn't solve her problems. She gave
herself up to the simple pleasure of shopping and soon
became enchanted by all the pretty, frivolous summer
dresses on the racks. And most of them were calling her
name. It was well after dinner when she got back to
Meadowlane. She had so many packages she decided to

leave them in the trunk of the car till she could get help
carrying them in.

Kirk was waiting for her in his study.

"Joanna, will you come in here, please?"

She sat in the chair across from his desk.

"You look very tired, Kirk. Did you work in the basement all afternoon?"

"No. I went to the office for a while. There were some
things I needed to take care of before my trip."

"Your trip?"

"Yes. I'm leaving tomorrow for Atlanta. There's a
matter at our Deerfield plant that can best be handled in
person."

"Isn't this rather sudden, Kirk?"

"Yes. But it's something I must do, Joanna." He picked
up two file folders, and handed one to her. "I haven't forgotten your day-care project. I've done some preliminary
work on it. Let's talk about it."

She and Kirk decided to convert a storage room on the
second floor. He gave her free rein on the project. Then on
Sunday morning, bright and early while she was still in
bed, he flew off, leaving behind an itinerary complete with
phone numbers in case of emergency.

Joanna hated the itinerary. It was so cold, so formal.
And it was a glaring reminder that Kirk was gone. She
couldn't see his face or hear his laughter or feel his hand
on hers. And she was bereft. For three days she dragged
around the house as if she were sick.

Even Rose commented on her behavior.

"It's not like you to mope around so. Maybe I ought to
call Miss Sophie."

"There's nothing Aunt Sophie can do. Besides that,
she's still at the summer house in Maine."

"Then maybe I ought to call Janet."

At the mention of her mother's name, Joanna went very still. Where was her mother now? she wondered. Rome? Paris? London? She didn't know. It had been weeks since that last card. Would Janet come if she were called? If she heard of her daughter's aching heart, would she care?

She willed herself to put those thoughts aside.

"There's nothing anybody can do," she said quietly.

"I bet if Mr. Kirk were here, *he* could do something. I've never seen anything yet that man couldn't handle."

Suddenly Joanna smiled. "Neither have I, Rose. This is just going to take a little time, that's all." She hugged Rose. "Thank you."

"I don't have the slightest idea for what, but you're welcome."

After her talk with Rose, the bounce came back into Joanna's step. She was glad the blues were behind her. She'd never wasted so much time feeling sorry for herself. She'd read somewhere that the course of true love never runs smoothly. She was beginning to believe that the course of true love was totally bewildering. Who would have thought that loving could cause the blues?

Joanna plunged into her work with renewed vigor, working long hours to get the day-care center going. Late one evening as she was painting rainbows and flowers on the walls of the center, Alfred came by.

"You look good in pink paint, Joanna." He touched a smudge on her cheek.

Joanna pulled back and reached for a cloth. She scrubbed vigorously at her cheek. "Hi, Alfred. How have you been?"

"Lonesome. *Where* have you been? Every time I call you at home, you're at the office. And when I call your office, you're up in the playroom. By the time I get to the playroom, you're gone. If I weren't so cocky, I'd be feeling neglected and abandoned."

"Don't be. I've been busy."

He glanced around the room. "I can see that. It looks good. The whole plant's buzzing about your project."

"I know. They're very excited, especially the working mothers."

"Speaking of work, Joanna, you seem to be doing nothing but that these days." He reached for her hand. "I miss you."

"I don't want you to miss me, Alfred."

"Such a serious face. Where's my playful scamp? Where's my charming frivolous playmate?" He squeezed her hand. "What's going on, Joanna?"

She tugged him toward a makeshift bench, two sawhorses with a board between them.

"Do you have time to sit beside me and be my friend?"

"That sounds omnibus." Alfred waggled an imaginary cigar in an exaggerated Groucho Marx imitation.

Joanna laughed. "Thanks, Alfred."

"For making you laugh? Any time. I mean that, Joanna." He chucked her under the chin. "Now, do you want to tell me what's going on?"

"Yes. I think I do." Joanna stared at the rainbow on the wall for a while before answering. "I'm in love."

"I believe you are. You should see your face right now. It's what the poets call glowing. Dare I ask if I'm the lucky man?"

"Oh, Alfred." Joanna gave him a quick hug. "You're such a nice person. I almost wish it were you."

"For several days now I've had a sinking feeling that I'm not the number one man in your life. Since our command lunch date, as a matter of fact."

"It's Kirk. I'm in love with Kirk."

"I was afraid you were going to say that." He smiled at her. "He's a good man, Joanna. A man of integrity and courage."

"I never meant to hurt you."

"I know that." He smiled. "And I don't think I'm mortally wounded."

"You're not even bleeding."

"I wouldn't dare bleed on your new day-care center." He became serious again. "Joanna, I wish you and Kirk all the happiness."

"It's a little early for that. Kirk doesn't even know I love him. And he's certainly never told me he loves me. As a matter of fact, I think he'd be horrified at the idea."

"Good lord, Joanna. It would take a man of iron to resist you."

"Sometimes Kirk Maitland is a man of iron. He's in Atlanta, and I haven't heard from him in over a week."

"You're sure about loving him?"

"Absolutely. It took me a while to recognize it, being the silly innocent I am; then I tried to deny it—for Kirk's sake more than mine. But I can no longer deny the truth. I want Kirk Maitland more than I've ever wanted anything in my life. I'm very much in love with him."

"Then take my advice; do everything in your power to get him. Love is a rare and beautiful thing. Don't let it slip away from you."

"Thank you, Alfred."

"That's what good friends are for—to give advice. It makes us feel wise and needed."

"You are."

"Which one?"

"Both."

"Lunch tomorrow? Just friends?"

"Yes. Lunch. Just friends."

* * *

The days slipped by, and still Kirk didn't call. Joanna fussed at her telephone every time she passed by. "Ring, darn it. Why don't you ring?"

She joined the Pet Lovers' Association, partly to help fill her time, partly out of a newly blossomed civic pride and partly to become the productive woman she believed Kirk wanted.

On Tuesday night she dressed for her first meeting. Just as she started for the door, the phone rang.

"Kirk?"

"How did you know it was me?" She heard his wonderful voice at the other end of the line.

"Wishful thinking." Her joy spilled over and she laughed. "Who says wishes don't come true?"

"What have you been doing, Joanna?"

"Missing you."

There was a long silence at the end of the line. If she hadn't heard his breathing, she would have thought they'd been disconnected.

"I've missed you, too, baby."

"Kirk, are you all right? Your voice sounds funny."

"I'm a little tired. I suppose I've been working too hard."

"When are you coming home?"

Again that long pause.

"Not yet. Not for another two weeks or so. Tomorrow I'm flying to our plant in Charleston. I've decided to make a whirlwind tour of all our branches. It's been too long since I've been in personal contact."

The news made Joanna feel dead inside. She clutched the receiver as if she wanted to strangle it.

"Joanna, are you still there?"

"I'm here."

"How's progress on the day-care center?"

"We'll be ready to open it in another day or two."

"That's good news." Another long pause. "Are you keeping busy otherwise?"

"I go out occasionally."

"With Alfred?"

"Yes. There's no need for you to promote his case with me. I know he's a good man, but I can never fall in love with him. And he knows it."

"Believe me, Joanna, promoting Alfred is the last thing I want to do."

"Then what motivated your question?"

"If I knew, Joanna, it would probably scare the hell out of me."

"Is that why you're staying away so long, Kirk?"

"Partially. I do need to make this business tour, but I also need time to sort some things out. Personal things."

"Marsha?"

"Dammit, no!"

"You needn't shout. I'm not hard of hearing."

"You're so innocent, Joanna. And so damned young."

"Being young and innocent isn't a crime. But being thickheaded should be."

"Who's being thickheaded, Joanna?"

"You."

There was a long silence at the other end of the line. Then she heard his voice again, calmer this time. "I didn't call to fight with you."

"I don't want to fight with you, either."

"You sounded so cheerful when you answered. What's happened to you?"

"What's happened to us, Kirk?"

"If I knew the answer to that, I'd be home instead of in this godforsaken hotel in Atlanta."

"Are you lonesome, Kirk?"

"Yes. I never knew the meaning of being alone until you came back to Meadowlane. I miss the sound of your laughter, Joanna. I even miss those cusswords you use every now and then when you think I'm not listening."

"I'll join you, Kirk. I can meet you in Charleston and tour the branches with you."

"No. I don't want that."

"It's my company, too."

"Point well made. I know I'm being arbitrary and dictatorial, but I can't let you join me."

She wanted to cry. She felt rage and frustration and love so strong it twisted her insides. Her knuckles turned white as she gripped the phone, biting back tears.

"Joanna? I'm sorry, baby. Don't be hurt. I don't want you ever to be hurt by me."

"It's a risk I'm willing to take, Kirk."

"I won't let you. Goodbye, sweet one."

By the time she could speak around the lump in her throat, the line was dead. He'd hung up. Joanna stood, holding the receiver in her hand. The pain she felt was physical. Her stomach felt tight and there was a dull throb at the back of her neck.

Love has many facets, she thought as she carefully cradled the receiver. She'd never known that one of them was pain.

She washed her face with cold water. When she got to Bel Air Center, the meeting was already in progress. And just her luck, Marsha Holmes was presiding. If Joanna had been a dog she'd have thrown back her head and howled. Seeing Marsha after that disastrous phone call from Kirk was adding insult to injury.

For about two seconds she considered turning around and going home. But she was no quitter. She wasn't about to give up without a fight—either Kirk or the Pet Lovers' Association. If it took her the rest of her life, she'd have Kirk. And if it took her from now till Christmas, she'd learn to tolerate Marsha Holmes, even if she did want to punch her every time she thought of her in Kirk's arms.

Sitting on a back-row seat, Joanna listened to Marsha tell about the work of the club and the proposed projects. Marsha was excited about the work and genuinely interested in the welfare of the animals. As she spoke, Joanna began to feel very small. Marsha was a delightful person, one she could have been enjoying all summer if she hadn't let her feelings get in the way. She decided that jealousy was a shallow, petty emotion, one totally unbecoming in an adult, and one she was putting behind her. Starting right now.

She smiled, imagining herself leaping over another of the hurdles labeled "womanhood."

After the meeting Marsha approached her.

"I saw you come in, Joanna. I hope this means you've joined the Pet Lovers' Association."

"I have. Since I'm probably going to make Tupelo my permanent home, I've decided it's time to start participating in civic activities."

"I'm glad you chose us. We need all the help we can get. Especially now. We're trying to raise twenty-five thousand dollars to build better kennels at our animal shelter. Our winter quarters are totally inadequate."

"I love animals, and I can't imagine any of them without proper shelter. How can I help?"

Marsha laughed "That's exactly what I wanted to hear, the voice of a willing volunteer. The projects committee is meeting at my house tomorrow night to discuss ways of raising money. Can you come?"

"Yes."

"Good." Marsha gave directions to her house on Clay-wood Place.

Marsha's house was stone and redwood with lots of glass, modern and sophisticated, set among a grove of pines. As Joanna pulling into the driveway, she thought the house looked like Marsha, cool and in control, qualities Kirk admired. The green-eyed monster threatened to raise its head, but Joanna firmly squashed it.

She pulled her raincoat close around her, opened her umbrella and went up the walk. Marsha greeted her at the door.

"You're prompt. I like that." Marsha held the door open wide.

"Am I the first to arrive?"

"Yes. It must be a family trait. Kirk is like that."

Joanna won another brief struggle with her monster. "We're family only by marriage."

"I don't think he ever mentioned that." Standing in her own hallway, with the sophisticated half smile on her face, Marsha had never looked more beautiful. Joanna could imagine the powerful appeal she must have for Kirk. The two of them were so alike, always in command. No wonder he had never mentioned that he and Joanna were only stepcousins.

"The weather has turned nasty on us. Let me hang your raincoat in the closet."

Joanna peeled out of her red silk raincoat and watched as Marsha opened the closet door. There in plain view was a man's raincoat, black, masculine, strong, exuding the power of its owner—Kirk Maitland. She'd have known the raincoat anywhere for it had been her Christmas gift to Kirk two years earlier. She'd bought it in Paris and had barely gotten it in the mail in time for Christmas. If she'd had any doubts, the handkerchief dispelled them. It hung from the pocket, white as pain except for the dark blue monogrammed *M* in the corner.

Joanna's sharp intake of breath was audible. Marsha gave her a keen look.

"Kirk's coat," she said matter-of-factly.

"I recognized it."

"I know." Once again her face lit with that cool, sophisticated smile. "My legal-eagle mind is always at work. It's a matter of no importance." She shut the door on the coat.

Joanna was glad. She didn't want physical evidence that Kirk was very much at home in Marsha's house.

"You're right. It's only a coat."

Further discussion on the coat was halted by the arrival of the rest of the committee members. The meeting was lively, as well as productive. Marsha saw to that. Even with the matter of the coat nagging her mind, Joanna admired the way Marsha controlled the meeting. Projects were selected, goals set, events scheduled. The meeting was superb and so were the refreshments—small pecan tarts, freshly baked by Marsha. She was a superwoman, something Joanna could never hope to be, something she wasn't even sure she wanted to be. There was a lot of comfort in being merely human, Joanna decided, in knowing that it was permissible to fail.

After the meeting was over Marsha touched Joanna's arm. "Do you mind staying for coffee?"

Curiosity overcame her desire to be out of the house that held Kirk's coat captive.

"No. Of course not."

She waited in the den while Marsha escorted her other guests to the door. When Marsha came back with two cups of coffee, she was sitting on the edge of an ultramodern black leather chair.

"Thank you for staying." Marsha handed her a cup and sat down on the sofa. "I'll get right to the point." She took a delicate sip of coffee, then watched Joanna over the rim of her cup. "I don't want any misunderstandings to stand in the way of a friendship between us."

"The coat?"

Marsha laughed. "Precisely. I'm glad you didn't try to pretend ignorance. I would have been disappointed. Kirk is always so forthright. Somehow I expected you to be the same way."

"I am. Seeing the coat shook me. But it's absolutely none of my business what the two of you do."

Marsha's laughter was a discreet silvery tinkle. "What we do is talk—and laugh. Kirk has a wonderful sense of humor."

Thinking of his evening with Celestine, the broomstick bombshell, Joanna smiled. "I know."

"We're friends, Joanna. I never meant our relationship to be more than that. And neither did Kirk. We've both had bad marriages, and we both have demanding careers."

Joanna nodded and sipped her coffee, waiting for Marsha to continue.

"Kirk left the coat here a few weeks ago. It was a rainy weekend, and something was bothering him. He's a man who keeps his own counsel. I never knew what it was and I never asked. Our friendship is like that. We're comfortable with each other, Joanna."

"It's odd that he never came back for the coat."

"Not really. He's a very busy man. Although I'm sure he knew precisely where he'd left it, I called his office to tell him. He said he'd call me sometime and come by to pick it up. With his busy schedule—and mine—that could be next fall."

"Thank you for telling me this, Marsha." Joanna put her coffee cup on the glass-top table beside her chair and stood up. "Honesty is a good way to start a friendship."

"I think so, too." Marsha led the way to the hall. "You have a stunning smile, Joanna. No wonder Kirk is so enchanted by it."

"He's enchanted?"

Marsha opened the hall closet and took out two raincoats—Joanna's and Kirk's. "Yes. He says angels stop work on rainbows to bend down and watch you smile."

"He's never poetic."

"About you he is. He speaks of you often, always with a deep sense of pride, as if he'd personally designed and manufactured you."

Joanna laughed. "He didn't do that, but he practically raised me. Kirk Maitland's been taking care of me since I was three years old."

"He'd be good at that. Very good, indeed." Marsha handed her the two raincoats. "You might as well take Kirk's. It could be a while before he's here again."

Joanna took the coats and draped them over her arm. The rain had stopped half an hour earlier. After bidding Marsha good night, she headed to her car, Kirk's black Lincoln. Inside the vehicle, she lifted his raincoat to her face and inhaled. It smelled faintly of Kirk's after-shave, a cool outdoors smell, like the forest after a rain. Sitting there in the dark, sniffing his raincoat, she didn't even feel foolish. She felt wonderfully alive, glowing with anticipation for things she'd only read or dreamed. And she felt very much in love.

''Please come home soon, Kirk,'' she whispered to the darkness. Then she started her car and headed north, home to Meadowlane.

Chapter Eight

Kirk didn't call Joanna again after he left Atlanta. It was purely selfish on his part. He knew he couldn't hear her voice again without catching the first plane home, and he knew he couldn't go home yet, not until he'd settled his personal dilemma.

In Charleston he took out other women, sleek, sophisticated women with degrees in law and science and mathematics, older women who knew all the rules and never made a move that wasn't calculated. His plan was to dine and dance with Charleston's brightest and best, then to finish the night in their beds in a pleasurable blur of wine and forgetfulness. It was a drastic and cowardly way of handling his problem, but he thought nothing less than complete debauchery would wipe Joanna from his mind.

He never got as far as the debauchery, he reflected later. He never even got as far as a kiss. Joanna kept intruding. Over the first candlelight dinner, he thought of her delightful revenge with Celestine. He spent the rest of the evening regaling his companion, the lawyer, with stories of Joanna's escapades. She was bored to tears. And rightly so. He took her home right after dessert and spent the rest of the evening in his hotel room reading the *Wall Street Journal*.

Determined to do better, the next two nights he'd taken his dates dancing. That had been a tragic mistake. All it took was a little imagination to believe he was holding Joanna in his arms. She was the only woman he'd ever really danced with, the only woman he *wanted* to dance with. Every song reminded him of her. He'd unintentionally insulted both his dates by calling them Joanna. The scientist had caught a cab and gone home on her own, and the mathematician had pleaded a headache and asked to be let out on the street in front of her apartment.

Thinking back on his attempts at escape, he decided there was no fool like an old fool. Nothing would wipe Joanna from his mind. He realized he was foolish even to try. He had to face his problem. He had to either let her go or try to keep her. The first would be heartbreak; the second would be tragedy. He remembered all too well the stings and lacerations he and Belinda had inflicted on each other, hurts heaped on because of the vast differences in their ages and philosophies.

He left Charleston, driving to the airport in a thunderstorm that matched his mood. The storm delayed his flight to Charlotte three hours. His briefcase held enough work to fill the first two, but the last hour was spent in serious thought. He made mental lists of the pros and cons of a union between himself and Joanna. The cons far outweighed the pros. Just as the storm lifted, he came to the agonizing conclusion that he must give up Joanna. He had to relinquish all claims to her. He had to step aside, emotionally as well as physically, and let her find happiness with the right man. He could sense that she was struggling with an attraction to him, the same attraction that draws an innocent moth to an age-old flame. She'd be burned. And he would never allow that.

As he boarded his flight, his heart was heavy. He'd finish his tour, he decided, then he'd go home and set Joanna free. No more out-of-control kisses, no more spontaneous skating parties, no more basketball games in the moonlight, no more sultry dances in the parlor, no more jasmine-scented good-nights.

The plane carried Kirk's body high above the clouds, in that wondrous space where sea gulls never fly; but his spirit was in the depths of hell.

He came back to Tupelo without fanfare.

It was four-fifteen when he landed, almost closing time at Deerfield, but he rented a car and went straight to the office. Joanna was there, just as he knew she'd be, standing in the middle of the newly furnished day-care center, her back to the door, an outlandish hat with huge paper roses on her head, a puppet in one hand and a magic wand in the other. Around her, an enthralled group of children listened to the story she was telling.

Smiling, Kirk leaned against the door frame and watched.

"... and the fairy princess waved her magic wand," Joanna was saying, waving her silver wand over the heads of the giggling children as she talked, "changing the shy frog into the bravest frog in the pond. Oh, thank you, fairy princess. You've made me the happiest frog in the pond. Now I can do anything I want to because you've given me courage. I am no longer afraid. It's magic." Kirk smiled as Joanna worked the frog puppet, using her best frog voice. Then she slipped into her fairy princess voice. "The magic is in believing in yourself, George Frog. You were always a brave, happy frog. But you were afraid. Don't ever be afraid, George Frog. Someone who cares is always watching over you. And with a last wave of her magic wand, the fairy princess disappeared into the clouds, calling as she went, be yourself, George Frog. Be yourself.''

Joanna took a deep bow, beaming at her small charges. The children applauded and yelled.

"Yeah, Miss J'anna.''

"Can I wear the hat now, Miss Dear Field?''

"Can I wave the magic wand over Frankie? He wants to see if I can take his freckles off.''

"Who's that man in the door? Your husband?''

Joanna whirled around. Her eyes widened, her face flushed, and her mouth tipped up in the most beautiful smile Kirk had ever seen. He wondered how he'd survived these last few weeks without Joanna's smile.

"Hello, Joanna. I'm home.''

"Kirk!'' She threw the puppet and the magic wand into the toy box and flew into his arms, still wearing her funny hat, hugging him so hard and close he could feel the runaway rhythm of her heart. Still holding him tightly around the chest, she tipped her head back and looked up. "I'm so glad to see you I could die.''

"A little drastic, don't you think?'' He selfishly wanted to hold her. He wanted to lean down and take those tender rosy lips. He wanted to bury his face in that delicate neck and inhale her fragrance. Instead he gently put her away and walked into the playroom, inspecting the changes she'd made. "You've done a good job, Joanna.''

A small girl with Oreo cookie crumbs on her face tugged at his sleeve. "Are you Mr. May Land?''

Kirk squatted beside the pint-size cherub. "Yes, angel. I'm Mr. Maitland. What's your name?''

"Sunny. My mama works in the sec'etary's pool, but she never brings her swimsuit to work. Can I swim in the sec'etary's pool?"

"Well, Sunny, the secretary's pool is not like an ordinary pool. People don't swim in that kind of pool."

"Why not? Don't you have any water?"

Kirk looked up to see Joanna holding back her laughter. "Help me out with this, Joanna. I'm not accustomed to dealing with anybody under the age of twenty-one."

The plant whistle announced five o'clock.

"Saved by the bell." Joanna bent down and put her arm around Sunny's shoulders. "Tomorrow I'm going to take you down to the secretary's pool and tell you all about it. How will that be?"

The cookie angel tilted her bright head to one side, considering the proposition. "If I can't swim in it, I don't want to go." Then she bounced off and became absorbed in her coloring book.

Joanna laughed. "How soon the young forget."

Kirk stood up, carefully putting some distance between him and Joanna. "The resiliency of youth is wonderful. I almost envy all of you."

"All of us?"

"Yes. These children. You."

Further conversation was halted by the arrival of the first mother to pick up her child. One by one they came, stopping long enough to express their appreciation and delight over the new day-care center.

At five-fifteen Joanna closed the door on the last small child and his grateful mother. Then she turned and went straight to Kirk's arms.

"I've missed you so."

He held on to her, telling himself it would be the last time.

"I've missed you, too, Joanna."

She pressed her cheek against his chest. "I never realized how desperately I'd miss you until you were gone. I felt incomplete without you."

As I did, without you, he wanted to say. He called on his sense of humor to try to control the situation. "If I'd known you'd feel that way, I'd have hired another dictator to take my place while I was gone."

She stepped back. The look she gave him reminded him of a bristling kitten. "That's not what I meant, and you know it."

He gazed at her a long time without answering. She returned his stare boldly. He admired her control, her dignity. The Joanna he was facing wasn't the same Joanna he'd left behind. There was a new maturity about her.

"You're right, Joanna. I know. I've known for some time."

"That's why you left Tupelo?"

"Yes. The first time I kissed you, I sensed your attraction for me. And my response to you shocked the hell out of me. What was happening between us got out of hand." He reached for her, then changed his mind and let his arm drop to his side. "It won't work, baby. I'm like George Frog. I can never be anyone except myself, a dedicated businessman whose life-style would bore you to tears."

"I don't expect you to be anyone else. I love you just the way you are."

"Don't say that. You're merely infatuated with me. You're young and innocent and at precisely the right age to become infatuated. I should never have let it happen. I blame myself. And proximity. The time was right for you and I was there."

"You have it all figured out, don't you?"

"Yes. I did a lot of thinking while I was away. And I blame myself for responding to you. You're a beautiful, desirable woman, and I reacted as any normal male would. But that doesn't excuse my behavior. I'm your guardian, your protector. I should have better control over my emotions."

"And what are those emotions, Kirk? Passion? Desire? Love?"

Looking deep into her eyes, he felt the familiar tug on his heartstrings, the powerful response of his body to hers.

"God help me, Joanna. I want you." He heard the sharp intake of her breath, saw the sudden pink in her cheeks. He tried to control his own ragged breathing. "I want you now," he whispered.

"Then take me. Love me. Teach me to love."

"I can't."

"Can't or won't?"

"Won't. I refuse to jeopardize your happiness by giving in to this selfish desire of mine."

"You have no right to make decisions about what will or will not make me happy. It's my life. I'm willing to take the risk."

"You're right, Joanna. I have no right to tell you what to do. I'm relinquishing control of your life. You don't need me anymore."

"Then why can't you love me? Why can't you let me love you?"

"There are a dozen different reasons. All of which you'd probably deny."

"That's not fair. You're not giving me a chance to build a case for us, to refute your reasoning. You're treating me like a child."

"I don't mean to."

"Then do me the courtesy of communicating with me."

"You're shouting, Joanna."

"I'm mad. I shout when I'm mad."

He smiled in spite of his turmoil. Thank God, he thought, some things never change. Joanna would always be a spirited, exciting woman. No man would ever subdue her and no man would ever tame her.

"That's one of the differences I was alluding to. You're as spirited as a newborn colt in spring and I'm a stodgy, methodical man. You enjoy travel and theater and dance and sports. I enjoy work. You once accused me of smothering you. And it's true. I'd smother you to death, just as I smothered Belinda."

"I'm not Belinda." She jerked off her hat and threw it across the room so hard the paper roses fell off. "Hellfire and damnation."

"Don't cuss."

"I'm not cussing. I'm venting my rage. Belinda has nothing to do with us. Why can't you forget about her?"

"Because my marriage happened. It's a part of my past. I believe a man should learn from his mistakes."

"Does learning from your mistakes mean never taking a chance on love again?"

"I won't take a chance with *you*, Joanna. You're too important to me—and I'm too old for you."

"Too old for what? Sex? I know darned good and well you have a libido. Do you think I'm too young and innocent not to know arousal when I feel it?"

His smile was bittersweet. "Not sex, Joanna. I'm too old in terms of philosophy and life-style. I'm accustomed to an orderly life. Little people like Sunny scare the hell out of me. I can't imagine myself surrounded by diapers and bottles and children who depend on me."

Her face softened. "You're afraid of failure, aren't you?"

"You've discovered my Achilles' heel. Failure is anathema to me. I *won't* fail with you."

"You have no idea how wonderful you are, do you? You're the finest, kindest, most generous, most compassionate man I've ever known. You're brilliant and assertive and successful and humorous and very much in control. One mistake is not failure, Kirk. I understand everything you've told me, but I don't agree with any of it. Give us a chance."

"I'm sorry, baby. I must live according to the dictates of my conscience. Logic and common sense tell me there can never be anything between the two of us except friendship. And so I'm setting you free."

"Don't..." She held up her hand as if to ward off the truth.

"I'll check into a motel tonight and move my things out of Meadowlane tomorrow."

"Meadowlane is your home, too. You don't have to move."

"Being in the same house with you would never work, and prolonging the move would merely prolong the pain. I'm so sorry, baby. I didn't mean to tell you like this. Somehow I imagined this discussion would be more civilized, less painful."

"Do you love me, Kirk?"

"Don't ask that. The question is irrelevant. My decision is made."

"Can you deny that you love me?"

She'd asked the one question he'd never answered, even to himself. He'd thought in terms of desire and passion and need, both his and Joanna's. In that lonely airport in Charleston, he'd even thought of marriage and its inevitable consummation. But love? It was the issue he'd avoided. Noble men gave up passion and desire and even marriage; but only cowards gave up love.

"I've never lied to you. I'm not going to start now." He captured her hand, felt it tremble in his. Tenderly he lifted it to his lips. "Yes. I love you . . . enough to let you go."

He released her hand and walked away, quickly, while he still could. The slamming of the door sounded like doom. A crash in the playroom announced Joanna's rage and frustration. His first reaction was to turn back and see if she had hurt herself, but he walked on resolutely. He'd released her emotionally. All that remained now was to free her financially. Tomorrow he'd go to the bank and place the bulk of her money under her control. Tomorrow he'd sever all the ties that bound them except the legal ones that couldn't be revoked—the business ties. Tomorrow he'd move out of Meadowlane.

He entered his office and locked the door. Sitting in his swivel chair, he stared out the window without seeing a thing. Tomorrow he'd be bereft.

After Kirk walked out of the playroom, Joanna cried. Her crying wasn't a delicate, ladylike sniffing; it was a sobbing, nose-reddening, messy affair. And she didn't even have a handkerchief with her. Leaving the playroom, she went down the hall to the ladies' room and blew her nose on a paper towel. It felt scratchy. The discomfort suited her fine. She didn't want to be comfortable. She wanted to be miserable, to wallow in her pain and rejection, to suffer with her broken heart.

Joanna spent ten minutes giving vent to her emotions, then she decided that crying would accomplish nothing except a headache and a red nose. She splashed her face with water, stuck her chin out at a defiant angle and went to get her purse. She wasn't licked yet. She knew darned good and well Kirk Maitland was too smart to give up somebody he loved. And he *did* love her. He'd said so. She'd just have to think of a way to make him see it.

As she was getting into her car, the words of the story she'd invented came back to her: "The magic is believing in yourself, George Frog." She sat on the front seat of the car—sweltering in the summer heat, totally unaware of the sprawling glass-and-concrete buildings, sublimely deaf to the clamorous sounds of traffic headed out of the city—and experienced her moment of epiphany. Kirk had fallen in love with a rambunctious, playful woman just as she'd fallen in love with a steadfast, authoritative man. It didn't matter that she wasn't cut out for big business, that she would never be like Marsha, that she preferred red cars to black and bangle bracelets to white collars.

"Be yourself, Joanna Deerfield," she said aloud. That's exactly what she'd do, she decided. She was a stubborn woman who fought for what she wanted. She'd fight for Kirk as fearlessly and recklessly as she'd fought for her independence when she first came to Tupelo. Her advantage now was that she was wiser. She understood passion and its power to control. Kirk had taught her that. She'd use that knowledge to win him back. Maybe she was being devious and unfair, but she didn't care. Given a choice between fighting dirty and losing Kirk, she'd fight dirty any day.

She put her car into gear and pulled out of the parking lot. She'd make Kirk change his mind, starting tomorrow. With that final avowal, she turned toward Meadowlane.

Kirk spent a miserable, sleepless night in a sterile, anonymous hotel room. Twice he almost headed to Meadowlane on a flimsy pretext, once to get a necktie he didn't need, and once to find a book on management techniques that had been sitting on his shelf unopened for three months.

For the first time in his life he questioned the wisdom of his decision. He'd released Joanna, but it didn't feel right. When it came to business, he'd always had good instincts, but they seemed to have failed him in this matter. How did he know she'd find happiness with another man? Hell, was there even another man he'd trust with her? How did he know somebody else wouldn't make her miserable? At least he would never hurt her intentionally.

Great flashes of hindsight kept him awake until almost three o'clock. The next morning he decided he looked exactly the way he felt, as if he'd been dragged through the pits of hell.

After forcing himself to swallow a tasteless breakfast of unidentified objects, he went to the bank and made the necessary moves to give Joanna financial independence. As a matter of caution and because he wanted to remain true to Grandfather Deerfield's trust, he set up her accounts so that she would have enough money to operate for a year without having to come to him. He decided that he would retain control of her investments. Then he found a modest furnished apartment on a street that at least had trees, and arranged for the transfer of some of his clothes.

Afterward he went to Deerfield. His first conference was with his manager, Whitman Harris. He had just finished the briefing when Joanna came into his office, unannounced, closing the door behind her. She was dressed in a flamboyant outfit of bright turquoise. Her bangle jewelry tinkled as she walked. She looked young and carefree, and if she were hiding a broken heart, he couldn't tell. He was foolishly disappointed, then he silently cursed himself for his selfishness.

"Good afternoon, Kirk."

"Hello, Joanna. How are you today?"

"Still living. The magazines say broken hearts don't kill. I've learned the hard way that that's true."

"I'm sorry, baby."

"Don't be. I haven't given up yet."

"Joanna."

"Don't worry, Kirk. I don't mean to chase you around the sleeper sofas and through the cafeteria, but I do mean to have you." He looked tired, she thought. She hoped that was an indication that he regretted his decision. Plumping up her resolve and her self-confidence, she perched on the edge of his desk, lifted her skirts and crossed her legs. The expression on Kirk's face pleased her. "I'm not above a little seduction and guile. This worked with Wexford; it might work with you."

"Behave yourself, Joanna."

Laughing, she hopped off the desk. "Scared you, didn't I?"

"No. You delighted me, as always. I'm having a hard enough time keeping my hands off you as it is. Will you please sit in that chair over there and be good?"

She sat in the chair across from his desk. "Way over here, Kirk? How mean of you. How can I seduce you from halfway across the room?"

He chuckled. "You little imp. I ought to pull you across my knee."

"You ought to lower me to the carpet and slip between my soft, satin thighs."

"Good lord, Joanna. Where did you learn such stuff?"

"In one of the steamy novels the nuns didn't know I had."

"You're still a rebel, aren't you?"

"Yes. But a rebel with a cause." Her bangle bracelets clanked as she reached into her purse and pulled out a

sheet of paper. "The very first thing I want to tell you is
that I hired a very competent woman to manage the day-
care center—June Lancelot. I interviewed her this morning. She comes highly recommended. She starts work next
week. The second thing is that I've pulled Evelyn from the
marketing department to fill in until June comes."

"I'm impressed, Joanna."

"I'm not finished yet." She consulted her notes. "While
you were gone I noticed some things that need changing.
The cafeteria has good food, but it's too sterile and func-
tional for real relaxation during a meal. These are my designs for revamping it." She pulled another sheet of paper
from her purse and tossed it onto his desk.

Giving him time to study the designs, she sat quietly in
her chair, watching him. She loved him so much she ached.
She loved the way his dark hair dipped over his forehead,
the way the fine laugh lines fanned out from his eyes. She
loved his hands, large, capable, strong. The urge to feel his
hands on her was so great she could almost taste it. Her
tongue flicked over her dry lips as she looked at Kirk and
hungered. All the mystery and wonder of first love coursed
through her, and she longed to bring it to fulfillment.

Once he looked up from the designs and smiled at her.
The memory of the night she sat in his study reading while
he worked returned to her. She remembered the passionate kiss, the desperate longing of her body. *I won't let you
deny us,* she thought. *I'll make it impossible for you to let
me go.* She lifted her chin in determination.

"These designs are excellent, Joanna. You have a real
talent."

"Thank you. I also have something else to tell you."

He studied her quietly. "Go on."

"The day-to-day operations of Deerfield Manufacturing are still beyond my comprehension. Even if I stayed

here for years, I would never learn to help run this company. My mind is perceptive, not analytical. My talents are creative, not managerial. I think the only real contribution I can make to this company is in fabric design."

She stopped, waited for his reaction, outwardly calm, a tornado inside.

"I never thought of that."

"That's because your thinking patterns are different from mine. To you, being a part of the company means having a command of balance sheets and financial statements."

"You're right."

"I've been studying the fabric designs we use on our line of sofa sleepers and our patio loungers. I think I can come up with some that are more modern, more exciting."

"What's your proposal, Joanna?"

"A design studio. Entirely on my own. With no obligation from Deerfield to buy from me."

He smiled. "You will, of course, give us first option on your fabric designs? A chance for you to be exclusive with us?"

"If that's what you want."

"It is."

"Then let's seal the bargain." She left her seat, came around the desk, and leaned over Kirk's chair. "My way." Her tongue traced his lips.

"My God, Joanna," he moaned.

The minute her lips touched his, her schemes were forgotten, replaced by an overwhelming need. She slanted her open mouth across his, savoring the taste of him. "Mmm. You're so delicious." With an effort she regained control, remembered her purpose.

Kirk's hand clamped on her shoulders and pushed her away. "This is insanity, Joanna. You don't know what you're doing."

"I know exactly what I'm doing. I'm proving to you that you're wrong." In spite of his hold on her, she managed to climb into his lap. Her arms slipped around his neck. "I know you love me, Kirk. Show me."

His eyes gleamed. "You *do* know what you're doing, don't you?"

"Yes. I'm an adult."

"No doubt about it."

Their awareness of each other fairly sizzled. They felt the magnetic pull, the compelling need to do something, anything to release the tension.

Looking deep into her eyes, Kirk spoke. "I've made my decision, Joanna. This dangerous game you're playing won't change that."

"I'll take that chance." She curved her hand around the back of his head and buried her fingers in his hair. "If you're afraid of a little adult kissing, say so and I'll leave. I can always find somebody else to teach me."

His mouth was grim as he rose from the chair. Slinging her over his shoulder caveman style, he stalked to the door and snapped the lock shut. With his hands on her waist, he let her slide down his body until her feet touched the floor. His eyes pierced hers as he pressed her back against the door. She felt the solid strength of his chest, the powerful muscles in his arms, the rigid passion he could neither deny nor disguise. "I'm selfish, Joanna. And possessive. If anybody is going to teach you what love is about, it's going to be me."

"I can hardly wait," she said softly.

"Be forewarned, Joanna. This does not mean commitment."

She gave him a Madonna smile. "Do you always do this much talking before you get to the good part?"

His mouth crushed savagely against hers. There was desperation in his kiss, and hunger and passion and the careful leashing of a man struggling for control.

When he finally lifted his head, his breathing was as ragged as her own. She knew she'd won a small first victory. But not the war. "Is that all?" she asked softly. "If it is, I've come to the wrong place."

His face was thunderous as his mouth came down on hers again. She felt the delicious intrusion of his tongue, the heady abrasion as he plundered the depths of her mouth. His ministrations were bold and thorough. A small whimper of pleasure escaped her, and she went limp in his arms.

Without breaking contact, he turned her around and walked her across the room to his swivel chair. Still keeping up that heady thrusting and probing with his tongue, he maneuvered them until he was in the chair and she was across his lap. They battled in the chair, each striving for control and supremacy. Her nerves were screaming as she fought to maintain the complete awareness that would give her the edge. Then suddenly her control shattered and a spasm of passion shook her. Kirk groaned deep in his throat as he, too, gave up the battle.

What was happening between them became as ancient as time and as simple as a smile.

Withdrawing his tongue, he whispered against her lips, "I love you, Joanna. I can never stop loving you."

"Then don't. Please don't."

She felt the tensing of his body, sensed his struggle.

"God help me, Joanna. I can't let you go."

"Take me, Kirk. Love me."

Lifting his head, he gazed down at her. His eyes probed hers, searching, seeking answers. She scarcely dared breathe. For a small eternity she waited. Suddenly she saw the change in him, saw the light come into his eyes, felt him relaxing. And she knew, as surely as if it were written on the wall, that Kirk was experiencing his moment of epiphany. Her joy spilled over in her smile.

"Always, baby," he whispered. "Always."

He spoke just that one word, in a husky, love-filled voice, but it was enough. She knew it was a pledge.

He lowered his lips to hers in a kiss that was free of any restraints. Nothing was held back. All the love, the passion, the need, was there in the kiss.

Slowly his mouth left hers and burned a trail down her throat and across the open neck of her dress. His hand expertly opened her buttons and nudged aside the lace of her bra. "You are a fever in my blood. I can't resist you," he murmured as he lowered his mouth to her breast. She felt the white-hot sensations rip through her as his tongue toyed with her erect nipple. "I have to taste you." He took the nipple deep in his mouth, suckling until she felt as if she were falling off the edge of the earth.

Instinctively she tangled her hands in his hair and pulled his head closer. "I never knew love could be so wonderful. I feel as if I'm floating."

"Joanna...Joanna." In a fog of passion he lifted her so that she was astride him, her legs on either side of the chair. "Oh, God, baby. Float with me." His lips took hers once more, held them captive while his hips gently initiated her to the rhythms of love. The swivel chair rocked under them. She could feel the rigid power of him, the compelling heat of him. Business suit against silk, steel against satin.

Joanna was almost delirious with the pleasure of discovery. She caught Kirk's rhythm, moved with it, flowed with it. His hot murmurings against her mouth inflamed her. "Oh, baby...yes...like that...Joanna...what you...do to me." The crazy rocking and squeaking of the swivel chair only heightened their excitement.

"Kirk!" His mouth muffled her plea. A savage, primitive need ripped her. She tore her mouth away from his. "Please, Kirk. I want ... I need ... do something."

He cupped her face and planted soothing kisses around her jaw. "I've been a selfish beast, baby. I'll help you."

He shifted her so that she lay in his lap. His hand slipped under her skirt, explored the soft, silky skin of her thighs. He stroked her, gentled her, murmured soothing words to her. "So good ... so ready." A ripple of incredible pleasure passed through her as his fingers slipped inside. She arched her head back and bit her lip to keep from crying out in ecstasy. With gentle persuasion he taught her the feelings of love. His fingers were magic, entering, withdrawing, entering, withdrawing, repeating the cycle until she felt a powerful clenching, a sudden release.

His mouth took hers once more. The kiss was tender, sweet. "Baby..."

Her eyes were bright, her face flushed. "I never knew love could be so wonderful."

"That's only an imitation. The real thing is a glorious ride to heaven and back."

"I want to take that ride. With you."

He smoothed back her hair, caressed her cheek. "How can I deny you, Joanna?" Lowering his head, he buried his face in her hair, inhaled the jasmine fragrance.

Silently he rocked her. She leaned against him, filled with contentment and a glorious sense of wonder.

"Kirk?"

"Yes, baby?"

"Don't let me go. Keep me forever."

His arms tightened around her. "Are you sure you know what you're asking?" The rocking continued. "You've never known real freedom."

"I don't want freedom. I want you."

He loosened his hold and rearranged her so that he could see her face. "It can't be that way, Joanna. You've never known anything except my control. We've lived together, worked together. If I take you now, I'd never know whether you loved me by choice or simply because you've never been free to do anything else."

"If there were a million men at my feet, begging to marry me, I'd still choose you."

"Today, Joanna, I set you free."

Her chin came up. "No. I don't . . ."

"Hear me out. You'll find enough money in your account to live in any style you choose for the next year. That includes buying yourself a car. I know how you hate mine."

"How do you know?"

"I heard you call the Lincoln a stodgy old-fogy car."

"I didn't mean for you to hear that."

"But I did, Joanna. It only confirmed my feeling that I'm too old for you. Even now I have to wonder."

Giving him a fierce look, she caught his lapels. "No, you're not. And I won't let you go. Do you hear that, Kirk Maitland?"

He smiled. "Loud and clear." Then his expression became serious. "Joanna, I did a hell of a lot of thinking last night after I left you. I realized that I'm not as sure about matters of the heart as I am about business matters. It occurred to me that I've made many mistakes with you. When you first came up with the idea of finding a husband, I should have known it was merely a bid for freedom. If I had given you financial independence then, some of this heartbreak might have been avoided.''

She caressed his cheek. ''You're not God, Kirk. You can't control everything.''

He gave her a rueful smile. ''I'm beginning to see that, too. I have a confession to make, Joanna. Allowing myself the right to be human, to make mistakes, feels damned good.''

''I'm glad.'' She pressed her cheek to his. ''Does this mean you're asking me to marry you?''

He chuckled. ''Your methods of persuasion are very powerful. But I'm still old-fashioned enough to believe the man should do the proposing.''

She draped her arms over his shoulders and put her nose against his. ''Go ahead. I'm listening.''

''Without prompting, Joanna.'' He laughingly set her back. ''I want you, Joanna. I want to marry you, to have a life with you, but I'm going to put some distance between us, give us time to see if what we have can survive.''

''That's fair enough. All I want is a chance.''

He smiled. ''You'll get that, baby. I promise you. Somewhere between the door and the swivel chair I realized I had to give us a chance. I'm going to court you in a proper manner, as any other lovesick swain would do.''

''Then prepare to be swept off your feet.''

''I think I'm the one who's supposed to do the sweeping.''

Kirk's intercom buzzed and his secretary's voice came over the speaker. ''Mr. Maitland, I'm calling to remind you of your conference with Mr. Lackey at two.''

''Thank you, Karen.''

Joanna stood up and smoothed down her dress. ''What a mess. When planning a seduction, always bring a change of clothes," she quipped. "I read that somewhere in a magazine."

"What sort of magazine..." Kirk caught himself and stopped, grinning. "Old habits die hard." He took her hand and pressed it to his lips. "Don't worry, baby. I'll call and have someone bring you a change of clothes."

"What about you?"

"I keep a change here at the office."

"For seductions in the swivel chair?"

"Strictly for business, Joanna."

He picked up the phone and dialed.

Chapter Nine

Joanna bought her car, a bright blue Jaguar. She set her studio up in the sunroom at Meadowlane, replacing the dining furniture with an easel, worktable and desk.

It took her only a week to accomplish her tasks. During that week, Kirk had kept his distance. Joanna understood and didn't press. He'd promised to court her, and she knew he would—when he decided the time was right. She found that she enjoyed her new freedom. She filled her time with sketching and her new charity, the Pet Lovers' Association.

On Saturday she got up early and headed for Westwood Park. The Pet Lovers' Association was having a pet show to raise money for the animal shelter. The show had been her idea. Unlike most animal shows, the pets didn't have to be purebred. Any animal would do. And all would get a ribbon. There would be categories for the ugliest cat, the shortest dog, the most bowlegged chicken, the rabbit with the longest ears. If an animal didn't fit the categories, Joanna would make up one.

Marsha was already there, setting up the registration booth.

"Hi, Joanna. You look perky today."

"I feel as if there's been a contest to pick the luckiest woman in the world, and I won the prize."

Marsha laughed. "Stand close to me. I want some of that luck to rub off."

"Tough day?"

"Tough week. Tough life. Sometimes I question my wisdom in choosing law."

"I'm sure the feeling will pass. Most bad feelings do."

"Thanks, pal." Marsha stacked the registration sheets on the table. "Here comes our first entrant. It looks like Frankie Meaders and his performing basset hound."

"What does it do?"

"When Frankie whistles 'Yankee Doodle' the dog howls."

"How do you know?"

"Because they live next door to me. Frankie just learned to whistle and that's the only song he knows. He practices constantly. You register him. I can't bear to give that dog a prize."

In the next half hour, Joanna registered Frankie's basset hound, three poodles, a Siamese cat and a big white goose named Myrtle.

"Hello, Joanna. Is this show just for children or can anybody register?" That familiar voice made her heart pound in a crazy rhythm. She jerked her head up, smiling.

"Kirk! How have you been?"

"Staying busy, biding my time."

Marsha, who had finished registering the last person in her line, joined the conversation. "I must be seeing things. Kirk Maitland at a pet show. What brings you out?"

"Hello, Marsha." he smiled in her direction. "I saw your ad. It clearly stated that you and Joanna would be registering pets. And so I've brought mine."

He picked up the small dog at his feet. Nobody had noticed the little animal. At the sight of Joanna, his tail wagged fiercely.

"You've brought Rags," Joanna said. "I'm so glad. You must have stopped by Meadowlane."

"Yes. I had to get a few of my things anyway, so I decided to bring our faithful friend over. I think he deserves a prize for eating your egg soufflé, don't you?"

Joanna's smile widened. "Indeed I do."

"Private joke?" Marsha asked. "Or can anybody join?"

"Not private," Kirk said. "One morning when I had practically ordered Joanna to eat, she defied me by feeding her breakfast to Rags."

Marsha chuckled. "Kirk Maitland, I believe you've met your match."

His smile was for Joanna only. She basked in the promise in his eyes.

"I believe I have," he said softly.

Marsha saw the look that passed between them. "Well now," she said, "suppose I let Joanna look after you? I see an approaching pig who will probably need my full attention."

While Marsha dealt with Kermit Granger and his pig, Squealer, Joanna turned her full attention to Kirk. Remembering the last time they'd been together, she felt flushed.

"I'm glad you came, Kirk—for the sake of the ani-mals."

"So am I." His eyes gleamed as they raked over her. "For the sake of the animals."

The huskiness in his voice and the look in his eyes made her want to haul him under the registration table and make love to him right in the middle of Westwood Park.

She flicked her tongue out and wet her lips. "It will cost you, of course."

He bent down to pick up the registration sheet and a pencil. "It already has," he said softly, for her ears only. "Seeing you without taking you in my arms has cost me ulcers."

She smiled. "I think something can be arranged."

"Are you asking me for a date, you brazen woman?"

"Yes. Total freedom is lonely."

"Relinquishing control is lonely, too, Joanna." He filled out the form as he talked. "Tonight?"

"Yes."

"Dinner at eight?"

"And later?"

"Who knows? It's been a long time since I've been in-volved in a sincere courtship." He grinned wickedly at her. "I'm not sure I can remember what to do."

"Most of the magazines suggest candlelight and cud-dling."

"I think we can improve on that, Joanna." He reached into his pocket and brought out a folded check. "I believe the fee goes to the animal shelter."

"Right. We're hoping to build better winter quarters."

"Rags and I are happy to make this contribution."

She unfolded the check and looked at the amount. It was for five thousand dollars. "Thank you, Kirk. I believe I can match that.'' She furrowed her brow as she tried to calculate the balance in her account. "Can't I?"

Kirk laughed. "You can more than match it, Joanna. You're set up so that you won't have to come to me for anything—unless you try to buy New York."

"Only if it goes on sale." As he laughed, she pointed in the direction of a roped-off arena. "You can take Rags over there with the other pets so the judges can give him a ribbon."

Kirk strolled off with Rags, whistling.

Marsha shook her head and leaned toward Joanna. "I don't believe what I'm seeing. Just look at him over there in that arena full of children. I've never seen him so relaxed. What in the world have you done to him, Joanna?"

"It's magic."

"It must be. The Kirk Maitland I know is a dedicated workaholic, like me."

They both watched as Kirk squatted down beside a small girl with a bobtailed beagle. He smiled and chatted with her as naturally as if he dealt with pigtailed five-year-olds every day.

"He looks so happy," Marsha said. "I'm proud for you, Joanna. I'm proud for both of you."

"Thanks."

Marsha laughed. "Forthright, as always. I almost wish you'd given me a silly denial. Kirk Maitland is one great guy. I could feel deprived if I thought about this too long."

"You're too smart to waste time on regrets."

"Exactly. Let's get on with this business of the pet show."

Joanna and Marsha registered the last of the pets and were stuffing the money into a bag when the bottom dropped out of the sky. Raindrops as big as tadpoles

poured over them, sending children and animals scurry-
ing in every direction. A great gust of wind whipped across
the lake and ripped the banners off the registration booth.

"I'll take care of the money," Marsha yelled as she ran
toward her car. "You grab the registration sheets."

Joanna started stuffing the sheets into her purse, glancing up now and then to see Kirk helping the two judges,
Glenna Rigsby and Letitia Blankenship, hustle the children and their pets to the shelter of a nearby pavilion.

Kermit Granger was anxious to go, but his pig had other
ideas. Squealer, excited by all the commotion and not
seeing anything that looked even remotely like a pigpen,
decided to be ornery. He planted his hooves in the mud and
balked right in front of the big white goose. Myrtle took
exception. She reached out with her beak and whacked
him on the tail. Squealer gave an outraged grunt and
scooted across the park, dragging little Kermit Granger
behind him.

As they passed Joanna's booth, Kermit yelled, "I can't
stop him."

Joanna set out after them with the goose in hot pursuit.
"Shoo. Go away," she yelled at the enraged goose as she
tried to catch Kermit and his runaway pig. "Let go of the
rope, Kermit. Let go!"

"I'll lose my pig."

"Don't worry. I'll catch him."

Kermit released his hold and the pig continued his run
for safety.

"Don't let Squealer get away," he yelled to Joanna.

Kirk saw what was happening and joined the chase.
"Hang in there, Joanna," he yelled. "I'm coming." He
managed to cut the goose off and head him toward the
lake. Myrtle flapped into the water and began swimming

sedately, as if she'd never even considered anything as gauche as attacking a pig.

With the goose problem out of the way, Kirk concentrated on reaching Joanna. She was topping the hill behind the merry-go-round. Using his long-forgotten skills from high school track days, Kirk caught up with her. She had her hands on the pig's leash.

"I can't hold him, Kirk," she yelled.

"I've got him." He grabbed the leash.

The pig was small but had the advantage of being low on the ground and surefooted in the mud. Kirk and Joanna lost their footing and went down. Kirk kept his grip on the leash while trying to break Joanna's fall. Man, woman and pig ended up in a tangled heap. Heedless of their predicament, the rain slashed down on them, adding insult to indignity.

Kirk lifted the pig off Joanna's lap. "Are you all right, Joanna?"

"Yes." She was sitting on his left leg. "Are you?"

"I don't think anything important's broken."

She looked at him and began to laugh. "You should see your face. You're covered with mud."

"I feel rather foolish. You're sitting there with a pig in your lap, and I'm sitting here thinking about making love. It must be that wet T-shirt."

"I'll have to remember to wear it more often."

"Without the pig."

"Definitely."

Keeping a firm grip on the pig, he leaned over Joanna. "There's no point in wasting an opportunity," he murmured as his lips brushed against hers. "Especially since everybody else is on the other side of the park."

"I agree. I've always wanted to be kissed in the park in the rain."

It was a sweet joining, a glad reunion after a week apart. With their battle armor finally thrust aside, there was nothing between them this time except the pig. The rain soaked them as they sat in the mud puddle and kissed. It lasted until their reluctant captive demanded attention in a high, squealing voice.

"If it weren't for that pig, I might have scandalized you right here in the park, Joanna."

"I might have let you."

Kirk helped her up, tucked the noisy pig under his arm and started back across the park. By the time they got Squealer back to his grateful owner, most of the mothers had come to pick up their children. Kirk took Rags from one of the judges, and he and Joanna saw the last of the children off.

Joanna patted Rags's wet head. "You're bringing him back to Meadowlane, aren't you?"

"Yes. Poor old fellow would have his feelings hurt if I sent him back with you. He's partial to the Lincoln. Besides, he's a little nervous from all the excitement. I don't want you driving with a nervous dog."

Joanna beat Kirk home by five minutes. She just had time to put the tea on before he drove up. It seemed strange to her that he rang the front doorbell. When she opened the door, he was standing there, holding Rags and smiling.

"You don't have to ring, Kirk. This is your home, too."

"Not now it isn't. It's yours, Joanna. I only use my key for emergencies, such as getting Rags for the pet show." He handed the dog to her.

"Aren't you coming in?"

"No." He smiled. "I have a big date tonight. I have to go home and get some of the mud off."

"I think you look good in mud. Your date must be a very picky woman."

"She's a very beautiful woman." He smiled tenderly at her. "Even with a dirty face."

"I'm making tea, Kirk," she said softly. "We could shower first."

"There's only so much temptation a man can bear, Joanna." He gave her a swift kiss. "See you tonight."

They ate by candlelight. Afterward they rode down the Natchez Trace to the Old Town overlook. The rain had stopped, and the earth smelled fresh and green. Shadowed by the tall pines, they danced with Joanna humming the tunes.

"You're glorious in the starlight, Joanna. I could spend the rest of the evening just looking at you."

"I have something better in mind."

"Will I enjoy it?"

"Why don't you try it and see?"

She stood on tiptoe and pressed her mouth to his.

"I enjoy it, baby," he whispered. "I plan to enjoy it for a long, long time."

And he did.

They didn't get back to Meadowlane until two o'clock. Joanna's face was glowing and her lips were love-pouted. Kirk left whistling.

He courted her gallantly. He took her to the ballet and the symphony and the theater. He took her to openings at the art gallery and to readings at the library. He took her to movies and to lakes and to zoos. And always he was careful to restrain his passion. Their kissing sessions were ardent and prolonged, but he set limits. He knew Joanna was young and innocent and vulnerable. He didn't want a repeat of what had happened in his office. He didn't want her to confuse sex with love. And he didn't want to fool himself, either. He had to be very sure that what he felt for Joanna was the kind of love that would last a lifetime. He wasn't about to make another mistake.

The last days of summer drew to a close. September brought a nip to the air that hinted of an early fall. Joanna and Kirk were coming home from a benefit dance for the American Cancer Society.

"Tired, Joanna?"

She leaned into the curve of his right arm. "Almost aching. I can't believe I danced every dance."

"Tupelo's young swains wouldn't let you alone. I'm afraid I was jealous."

She turned and smiled up at him. "Were you?"

"Yes. Enough to cut in so that nobody had his hands on you too long. I'm not accustomed to the pace you set, Joanna. Every bone in my body aches."

She patted his face. "Poor sweet thing. I know just what you need."

"What?"

"The hot tub."

"Sounds tempting. But no thanks."

"There's no reason for you to do without that luxury simply because you're in some dinky little apartment."

"It's actually quite comfortable, Joanna—if I remember to suck in my stomach so I can get between the refrigerator and the kitchen table." He laughed so she would know he was teasing.

As he turned into the winding driveway that led up to Meadowlane, he changed his mind about the hot tub. One of his suits was still in the bathhouse. He was already in the warm swirling water when Joanna joined him. She was wearing a gold bikini hardly big enough to hold a sneeze. His arousal was instantaneous. He was thankful for the cover of the water.

Joanna stood on the edge of the hot tub.

"The water feels great, Joanna. Join me."

"Not yet." Her smile was delightfully wicked. He watched in fascination as she reached for the hook on her swimsuit bra. "In Spain," she drawled, "we consider the nude body a work of art." The wisp of gold drifted to the concrete. Kirk drew in his breath at the sight of her. Her breasts were luminescent in the moonlight, the glowing mounds tipped by nipples deep rose and proudly erect.

His eyes feasted on her, savored her luscious beauty. "In Tupelo we consider the nude body a blatant invitation."

He reached up and pulled her into the swirling waters. "You temptress." He set her squarely on his lap. Her eyes widened. He chuckled. "Play with fire, you're liable to get burned."

"It can't be soon enough to suit me." Dipping her hand in the warm water, she splashed her torso, leaning back so Kirk could watch the water slowly trickle over her breasts. "So...burn me," she said softly.

And he did. He devoured her lips, her breasts, holding her astride, plunging against her in the water until they were both breathless. When it was over he held her loosely against his chest.

"The next time there will be no swimsuits between us."

"Hallelujah."

"I had meant to give us more time, but under the circumstances that seems foolish."

"Wasteful," she agreed.

"I'd meant to do this with candlelight and roses."

"The answer is yes."

He chuckled. "I haven't even asked the question yet, you delightful little hoyden."

"I'm waiting."

"Will you marry me, Joanna?"

"I thought you'd never ask. Yes, yes, yes. When?"

"I'll call Dad and Sophie tonight. As soon as we can get them back from their summer place, we'll be married."

"We have to locate Mother."

"You want her, then?"

"Yes. I've always wanted her."

Kirk's stomach clenched with anger. He wanted to curse the woman who had abandoned Joanna, but he knew that doing so would further hurt the woman he loved. He pulled her closer, caressing her back, expressing his sympathy and support in the only way he knew.

Joanna put her cheek against his chest. "I used to think I'd done something to make her leave, but I know that's not true. Grandfather Deerfield explained to me that Daddy was Mother's anchor, that after he died she just seemed to drift away from everything and everybody." She lifted her head and looked at him, her eyes bright with unshed tears. "I know she hasn't been much of a mother, Kirk, but she's the only one I have—and I need her."

"Then you'll have her, baby." Kirk caught Joanna fiercely to his chest, vowing that he'd find Janet and get her to Tupelo even if he had to go and personally escort her home.

Kenneth and Sophie Maitland flew home the day after Kirk's phone call. They were delighted with the news. But Janet Deerfield was not. She flew in from Paris six days later and they all gathered at Sophie's house, bringing Janet up to date on the wedding plans.

"We've planned a quiet wedding," Kirk told her. "Family and a few friends."

Holding on to his hand, Joanna smiled. "Yes. Nothing that will take a lot of time and planning. A simple wedding in Aunt Sophie's rose garden. We've set Saturday morning as the date."

"Saturday morning." Janet jumped up from her chair and began to pace and talk, punctuating her complaints with jabs of the cigarette she held in her hand. "Impossible. I have friends in Paris who can't possibly get here in time. And what will everybody say, anyway? A Deerfield marrying in such a hasty manner. No engagement parties, no bridal teas. There'll be talk. Cousins marrying. It's simply unthinkable." She whirled on Joanna. "I'd always pictured you marrying somebody exciting on the continent. I'm simply too devastated by this news to know what to do. I might not even be up to coming."

Joanna's chin came up. "Mother, what you want is entirely immaterial to me. I've made my choice. The wedding is Saturday, whether you come or not."

After abandoning Joanna to the care of others, Kirk thought, Janet flies in and tries to ruin the biggest moment in her daughter's life. Kirk was furious, but knew he had to remain cool for Joanna's sake. He squeezed Joanna's hand. "Janet, we want you there, but we'll understand if you can't come. Under the circumstances, it might even be better for everyone if you don't. I won't have Joanna's wedding day marred."

Sophie rose from her chair and faced her former sister-in-law. Her control was perfect. Only the bright spots of color on her cheeks betrayed her anger. "Kenneth," she said quietly, "would you mind taking Kirk and Joanna into your study? I have a few things to say to Janet."

Kirk and Joanna followed Kenneth out of the room.

"I think I'll go into the rose garden," Joanna said. "I need some air."

"I'll come with you," Kirk said.

"No." Seeing the tight, worried look on his face, she stood on tiptoe and kissed him. "Don't worry. I just want to be alone for a while."

Kenneth and Kirk watched her go, then they went into the study. Kenneth poured two brandies and handed one to his son.

"Sophie will handle everything, Kirk. Don't worry."

"I have the utmost confidence in Sophie, Dad. But damn her frivolous hide, Janet did have a valid point. One I've considered myself."

"Cousins marrying?"

"Yes. No matter how sophisticated we think we are, Tupelo is still a Southern town with enough old-fashioned morality to create a stir about this wedding. I can handle it, but I don't want Joanna to be hurt."

"Son, you underestimate your bride-to-be. She's like her granddaddy, capable of handling anything. I think you also underestimate this town. In this day of divorce, nontraditional families are almost the rule rather than the exception. Stepcousins, even stepbrothers and sisters marry. There won't even be an eyelash batted."

"Not even Gracelyn Phillips?"

Kenneth laughed. "Not even her." He held out his glass. "I propose a toast. May your marriage to Joanna be as happy as mine to Sophie."

"I'll drink to that."

The wedding was a quiet, lovely affair. The weather cooperated beautifully, and so did Janet. Whatever Sophie had said to her had worked, Kirk decided. With the potential problem eliminated, he turned his full attention to his bride.

He'd always heard brides were radiant, but his looked as if she'd just stepped down from heaven. Dressed in white, she was an angel, *his* angel. As she came toward him through the rose garden, he said a prayer of thanksgiving for second chances. Taking her hand, he pledged his vows before God and man to love and cherish her—forever.

After the wedding, the Maitlands and Janet hosted a celebration party. Amid all the jokes and backslapping, Mr. and Mrs. Kirk Maitland slipped away quietly.

Kirk fitted his key into the front door at Meadowlane and carried his bride across the threshold.

"Welcome home, Mrs. Maitland."

"I like the sound of that. Say it again."

He kicked the door shut behind them and nuzzled her neck. "I love you, Mrs. Maitland."

"Show me," she said softly.

His eyes caught and held hers as he carried her up the stairs. The only sound in the house was Kirk's feet on the wooden floor. With his wife in his arms, he made his way down the upstairs hall to the enormous master bedroom. The huge brass bed gleamed in the rays of the late-afternoon sun.

Joanna swung her eyes from Kirk to the bed and back. "A real ride this time?"

"To heaven and back."

He lowered her to her feet. His eyes never left hers as he reached around and began to undo the buttons on her wedding dress. Ever so slowly, he slipped the satin from her shoulders and watched it fall into a pool at her feet. Joanna stood before him in a white lace teddy and white satin heels.

"Have I told you lately that you're the most beautiful woman in the world, Mrs. Maitland?"

"Not lately, Mr. Maitland." She drew in her breath as he reached out and traced her body with his hands. Taking his time, he let his fingers drift over her smooth tanned shoulders, down her arms. He lifted her hands, one at a time, and tenderly kissed each palm. Then his hands explored her breasts, moved down her flat stomach and rested on her warm femininity.

Stepping back, he took off his shirt, let it drift to the floor. "Come here, baby." His voice was a husky whisper. He slid the straps from Joanna's shoulders and pushed away the top half of her teddy, exposing her breasts. With his hands on her shoulders he guided her to his chest, pressed her there. Slowly, sensuously, he began an erotic circling movement. His chest hairs gently abraded her nipples, causing them to jut in tight hard points. Lowering his head, he took one nipple into his mouth, sucking until Joanna moaned.

She arched against him. "Kirk, please."

"Easy, baby. Go slow." He ministered to her other breast, murmuring love words to her.

When she thought her legs would collapse, he lifted her and carried her to the bed. Leaning down, he slipped off her shoes. Then he peeled away her white teddy. A slanting ray of sunlight turned her body gold. He traced every inch of her with hot, tender kisses.

As his lips touched her skin, her head moved from side to side on the pillow. She ached and writhed, tense, waiting. She didn't know when he got out of his clothes, but suddenly he was lying beside her, his warm, hard body pressed close to hers. He took her hand and guided it downward.

"Touch me, Joanna," he commanded. "Know me."

Her hand trembled on him. She had the sensation of touching a steel rod encased in heated satin. With his hand on hers, he guided her, taught her. Her movements were tentative at first, than she was boldly caressing him.

Sweat popped out on her brow. She felt as if she were shattering inside. Unconsciously she grabbed Kirk around the chest and began a small rhythm against him with her hips.

"That's it, baby," he said softly. "Go with it." His fingers slipped into her, led her on. Her rhythms became quick and hard, and she was panting. "Slow, baby, slow. Take your time."

Her fingernails bit into his flesh and she cried out his name. "Kirk!" He eased his fingers out of her as she relaxed against him.

He soothed her, pressed his lips against her forehead, gently massaged her back. "Easy, baby. That's just the beginning."

She was completely relaxed when he moved her under him. Keeping his full weight off her, he took her mouth. There was a languorous quality to their kissing. Gently, Kirk parted her thighs.

"Love me, Kirk."

Her soft whisper was all the invitation he needed. Lifting her hips, he slid easily into her warmth. He smiled as her eyes grew big and luminous.

"Oh, Kirk. I never knew."

"I'm glad, baby. I'll be your first." He eased back and forth in slow strokes, then gently pressed through her maidenhood "And your last," he whispered.

With tender care, Kirk Maitland consummated his marriage to Joanna Deerfield. He led her slowly through the first stages of love, taught her the feel of flesh against flesh. Her passion and need kept pace with his. Together they escalated until she was wild under him. Keeping them joined, he flipped to his back, firmly holding on to her waist.

Her throat gleamed in the waning rays of sunshine as she threw back her head and abandoned herself to love. Joy rocketed through her along with pleasure greater than she'd ever known. Kirk encouraged her with hoarse commands.

"Go with it, love deeper that's it . . . oh, God, Joanna." His powerful thrust sent the sun shattering and melting through her body. She clenched around him, holding him deep inside as he spilled his seed. Their combined cries of release rang out in the bedroom.

"You are truly magnificent, Mrs. Maitland." Kirk pulled her down onto his chest and caressed her hair.

"The best, Kirk?"

He chuckled. "Without a doubt, baby. The very best."

She lifted her head and smiled at him. "I'm glad. Suddenly I'm jealous of your first wife and of . . ."

He shushed her with a long kiss. After it had ended, he held her face between his hands. "Joanna, my love, I plan to keep you too busy to be jealous."

"How busy is that, Kirk?"

His hips began a small rhythm. "I've always believed that showing is better than telling."

Turning her onto her back, Kirk Maitland showed his wife exactly how busy she'd be.

They slept till noon the next day, then drove to the Tennessee-Tombigbee Waterway in Fulton. A brand-new forty-four foot Hatteras yacht was docked there. The *Joanna* gleamed in the sunshine, white as a bride, awaiting her maiden voyage.

"Is this the surprise you've been keeping from me?" Joanna asked.

"Yes." Kirk took her hand and led her aboard. "My wedding gift to you."

Joanna fully understood the significance of the gift. That Kirk had chosen an expensive present didn't surprise her at all. He was generous, as well as wealthy. That he had chosen a yacht was astounding. Boats were a leisurely means of travel, generally owned by people who led rather carefree lives.

She threw her arms around his neck. "It's magnificent, Kirk. Thank you."

"You're welcome, baby."

Her mouth found his for a proper thank-you that threatened to become a lengthy session below decks. Finally she pulled back, laughing.

"No wonder you told me to pack nothing except play clothes."

"I intend to see that you do lots of playing on this honeymoon."

"With you?"

"Only with me." He kissed the top of her head. "You know what this gift means, don't you, Joanna?"

"Yes, Kirk, but I want to hear you say it."

"You've taught me that there's more to life than work. With you at my side, I believe I can achieve a balance between work and play. I will never again become so involved in business that I lose sight of the really important things in life."

"Such as?" she prompted softly.

"My wife, my marriage, my children."

"Kirk?"

"Hmm?"

"Do you think we can start practicing making one of those children right now?"

"I thought you'd never ask."

He led her below, drew the curtains, and obliged. Much later he said, "I think this is going to take lots of practice, Mrs. Maitland."

"So do I Mr. Maitland. When's the next practice session?"

"Minx." he gave her a love pat on the backside. "Upsy daisy. If these two old sailors don't heave to, we'll never get to Aberdeen, let alone the Caribbean."

"The Caribbean, Kirk? How long is this honeymoon going to last?"

"Forever." He found their scattered clothes and tossed them onto the bed. "The cruise part is going to last three months." Seeing her look of astonishment, he laughed. "The company is in very good hands. Whitman Harris is an excellent manager. And he's relieved to finally get a chance to prove his worth."

They dressed and went topside.

"Do you still remember your boating skills, Joanna?"

She laughed. "How can I ever forget? Grandfather Deerfield drilled us both until we would have done the U.S. Navy proud."

"That's what I was hoping. It would have been rather awkward to have to run out at the last minute and hire a boat crew to go along on our honeymoon."

"And much too crowded."

The *Joanna* got underway, cruising majestically down the man-made canal, through the Tombigbee River and into the string of lakes along the Mississippi-Alabama state line. Three leisurely days later they entered Mobile Bay and headed out into the gulf.

Far out on the gulf, with nothing around them except endless stretches of water, they dropped anchor. With the sunset washing them in gold and red and purple, Kirk took Joanna into his arms.

"It's been far too long, Joanna. Shall we go below?"

"I have a better idea, Kirk."

Stepping back from him, she unhooked her strapless halter and let it drop to the deck. He came toward her, smiling. Hooking his thumbs into the waistband of her shorts, he slithered them down her legs.

"I'm crazy about your ideas." He stepped out of his shorts and lowered her to the deck.

She tangled her hands in his hair and pulled him down to her. "Shall I tell you the one I have for Deerfield?" She was laughing when she said it.

"Later, baby. The company can wait. I can't."

The boat rocked gently with the rhythm of waves and the rhythm of love as Kirk and Joanna found ecstasy.

Epilogue

The invitations lay open on the hall table. *The Faces of Love, paintings by Joanna Maitland. You are cordially invited to meet the artist at a reception hosted by her husband, Kirk Maitland. Tupelo Art Gallery. 211 Main Street. Friday, March 15. 6:00-8:30 p.m.*

"Mrs. Maitland." Joanna turned from her easel. Her personal maid, Kristen, was standing in the doorway, holding a gold lamé dress. "This just came from the cleaners. Shall I lay it out for tonight?"

"That's fine, Kristen. Has Kirk come home yet?"

"Not yet, Mrs. Maitland."

"Let me know the minute he does."

Joanna worked forty more minutes, putting the finishing touches on the watercolor she was doing. It was a scene from Sophie's rose garden, the pink and white flowers seemed to bloom on the canvas, complementing the angelic pink-and-white face of a small child bent over, inspecting the delicate petals of the rose.

At precisely five o'clock, Joanna laid down her brushes and went upstairs. She bathed and dressed carefully. Tonight was a special night for her. In the past ten years, she'd achieved some success with her design business, but this was her first venture into painting. The showing at the art gallery would be her debut into the world of art.

She slipped the gold dress over her head and arranged her red hair into a sophisticated French twist.

Kristen's voice came over the intercom. "Mrs. Maitland, Mr. Maitland is home."

"Thank you, Kristen."

Leaving her bedroom, she waited for him at the top of the stairs. Her cheeks flushed pink as she heard his footsteps on the polished wooden floor, heard his deep voice speaking to Kristen. In the ten years of their marriage, she'd never failed to respond to the sound of his homecoming. Each time was like the first. She felt the same thrill, the same excitement, the same sense of anticipation.

"Kirk." The minute he came into view, she called out his name.

He lifted his head and stood at the foot of the stairs, gazing at her.

"Am I seeing a vision?" he asked softly. "Is that an angel dressed in gold at the top of my stairs?"

Her smile was as bright as her dress. "I'm real."

He put one foot on the stairs. "How can I be sure?" He never took his eyes off hers as he put the second foot on the staircase.

"Come up and touch me."

He moved toward her deliberately, taking his time, drawing out the moment until the anticipation was zinging between them like the too-tight strings on a violin.

"After all these years, you still have the most marvelous ideas."

She lost her breath as he took the last two steps at a bound and scooped her into his arms.

"Miss me, Joanna?"

"Desperately, Kirk. The last eight hours of my life have been empty without you."

"Then I shall have to make up for it." He carried her into their bedroom and kicked the door shut. His lips came down on hers. She molded herself to fit his familiar hard body. She could feel his need pressing against the front of her gold dress.

She drew back from him. "Kirk?"

He was already unzipping her dress. "I figure if I can dress in five minutes, we have the next half hour all to ourselves." Hairpins scattered across the carpet as he backed her toward the bed.

She unbuttoned his shirt. "Why let this golden opportunity pass us by?"

"My sentiments exactly." His belt buckle thumped against the carpet.

She sighed as he entered her. "Kirk Maitland, if I live to be a hundred, I'll never get enough of you."

"Nor I of you."

Talking ceased as Joanna gave her husband a proper welcome home.

Afterward, they laughed like giddy teenagers as they hastily dressed for the art gallery. Sitting in the back of their chauffeur-driven limousine, they put on the finishing touches. Joanna put Kirk's cuff links in and straightened his tie, and he tucked a stray curl into her French twist and finished zipping her dress.

When they emerged from the limousine, they were as cool and smiling as if they'd spent all afternoon getting ready for the event.

Together they greeted guests and ushered them on tours of the paintings.

One beautiful watercolor pictured a nine-year-old boy standing on the deck of a white yacht.

"Our oldest son, Mark," Kirk explained. "He's quite a sailor. Takes to the water as if he were born to it."

Joanna gave her husband a secret smile. Mark had been conceived on their honeymoon.

The next painting was in oils, a young girl bent over her desk, her dark hair falling halfway into her dark eyes.

"Eight-year-old Becky," Joanna said. "She's already showing an interest in the *Wall Street Journal*."

Two small red-haired children smiled down from the third canvas. They were bending over an ancient little dog.

"Kathryn and Andrew," Kirk said. "Our two youngest. Kathryn is the only six-year-old who ever managed to register her dog for first grade. Like her mother, she has a smile that nobody can deny. And three-year-old Andrew has already charmed his nursery school teacher into letting him take his pet frog to school."

Gracelyn Phillips turned from the painting to the proud parents. "And where are the children tonight? Will they be here?"

"They're with my mother. They'll all put in a brief appearance, and then she'll hustle them off to her apartment where she spoils them rotten."

Gracelyn's eyebrows shot up into her lacquered bangs. "Janet Deerfield? I thought she was living in Paris."

Joanna laughed. "Grandmotherhood transformed her. I think her wanderlust days are over."

Gracelyn shook her head in disbelief and turned to view the large watercolor that dominated the exhibit. Kirk Maitland, in a white open-neck T-shirt and casual slacks, sat in a chair on the front porch at Meadowlane, surrounded by his four children.

"This one is my favorite," Joanna said. "All the faces of love are here."

Kirk put his arm around her shoulders. "I think that's them just coming through the door."

Janet Deerfield, looking every inch the proud grandmother, led her four grandchildren into the art gallery. Within five minutes they were the center of an admiring crowd.

Janet walked up to her daughter and circled her arm around her waist. "My dear, you should have made me a grandmother twenty years ago. I'm having the time of my life."

Joanna laughed. "Twenty years ago I was only a teenager."

Janet waved her hand about in the air. "One forgets these small details." Her gaze swept around the gallery. "Speaking of small details, Joanna, there's something missing from these paintings."

"What, Mother?"

"A baby. The Faces of Love won't be complete without a baby."

"Joanna's working on that," Kirk said. "We have a large collection of photographs."

Joanna smiled up at him. "Yes. I'm working on it, but not from photographs."

"Well, it's about time," Janet said. "Little Andrew thinks he's too big to cuddle anymore." She patted Kirk's cheek. "For virility, you've surpassed kings." Smiling, she walked off to join her grandchildren.

"Joanna?" His voice was a soft question.

"Not yet. But I do think five is a nice number, don't you?"

"Indeed."

"If we start right away, maybe we'll make it by Christmas."

He smiled down at her. "Here? In the gallery?"

"Seeing you under the lights does put a certain idea into a girl's head." She laced her arm through his and led him toward a small group waiting for their tour. "But I suppose it will have to wait."

It waited until they were in the limousine. Kirk pushed the button that raised the partition between them and their chauffeur.

"With any luck, it will take us twenty minutes to get home," he said as he lowered her to the seat.

Joanna sighed. "Thank goodness for tinted-glass windows."

*   *   *   *   *

Silhouette Desire®

1989
IS THE YEAR
OF THE MAN!

What makes a romance? A special man, of course, and Silhouette Desire celebrates that fact with *twelve* of them! From Mr. January to Mr. December, every month has a tribute to the Silhouette Desire hero—our **MAN OF THE MONTH!**

Sexy, macho, charming, irritating . . . irresistible! Nothing can stop these men from sweeping you away. Created by some of your favorite authors, each man is custom-made for pleasure—*reading* pleasure—so don't miss a single one.

Mr. January is Blake Donavan in RELUCTANT FATHER by Diana Palmer
Mr. February is Hank Branson in THE GENTLEMAN INSISTS by Joan Hohl
Mr. March is Carson Tanner in NIGHT OF THE HUNTER by Jennifer Greene
Mr. April is Slater McCall in A DANGEROUS KIND OF MAN by Naomi Horton
Mr. May is Luke Harmon in VENGEANCE IS MINE by Lucy Gordon
Mr. June is Quinn McNamara in IRRESISTIBLE by Annette Broadrick

And that's only the half of it—
so get out there and find your man!

Silhouette Desire's

MAN OF THE MONTH . . .

MOM-1

Silhouette Classics

COMING IN APRIL...

THORNE'S WAY by Joan Hohl

When *Thorne's Way* first burst upon the romance scene in 1982, readers couldn't help but fall in love with Jonas Thorne, a man of bewildering arrogance and stunning tenderness. This book quickly became one of Silhouette's most sought-after early titles.

Now, Silhouette Classics is pleased to present the reissue of *Thorne's Way*. Even if you read this book years ago, its depth of emotion and passion will stir your heart again and again.

And that's not all!

Silhouette Special Edition

COMING IN JULY...

THORNE'S WIFE by Joan Hohl

We're pleased to announce a truly unique event at Silhouette. Jonas Thorne is back, in *Thorne's Wife*, a sequel that will sweep you off your feet! Jonas and Valerie's story continues as life—and love—reach heights never before dreamed of.

Experience both these timeless classics—one from Silhouette Classics and one from Silhouette Special Edition—as master storyteller Joan Hohl weaves two passionate, dramatic tales of everlasting love!

CL-36

Silhouette Special Edition

NAVY BLUES
Debbie Macomber

Between the devil and the deep blue sea...

At Christmastime, Lieutenant Commander Steve Kyle finds his heart anchored by the past, so he vows to give his ex-wife wide berth. But Carol Kyle is quaffing milk and knitting tiny pastel blankets with a vengeance. She's determined to have a baby, and only one man will do as father-to-be—the only man she's ever loved...her own bullheaded ex-husband!

You met Steve and Carol in NAVY WIFE (Special Edition #494)—you'll cheer for them in NAVY BLUES (Special Edition #518). (And as a bonus for NAVY WIFE fans, newlyweds Rush and Lindy Callaghan reveal a surprise of their own....)

Each book stands alone—together they're Debbie Macomber's most delightful duo to date! Don't miss

NAVY BLUES
Available in April,
only in *Silhouette Special Edition*.
Having the "blues" was never
so much fun!

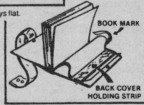

Silhouette Intimate Moments®

Let Bestselling Author
KATHLEEN EAGLE
Sweep You Away to
De Colores Once Again

For the third time, Kathleen Eagle has written a book set on the spellbinding isle of De Colores. In PAINTBOX MORNING (Intimate Moments #284), Miguel Hidalgo is all that stands between his island home and destruction—and Ronnie Harper is the only woman who can help Miguel fulfill his destiny and lead his people into a bright tomorrow. But Ronnie has a woman's heart, a woman's needs. In helping Miguel to live out his dreams, is she destined to see her own dreams of love with this very special man go forever unfulfilled? Read PAINTBOX MORNING, coming this month from Silhouette Intimate Moments, and follow the path of these star-crossed lovers as they build a future filled with hope and a love to last all time.

If you like PAINTBOX MORNING, you might also like Kathleen Eagle's two previous tales of De Colores: CANDLES IN THE NIGHT (Special Edition #437) and MORE THAN A MIRACLE (Intimate Moments #242).
